# LOOKING FOR MR. WRONG . . .

"Let's take out interesting," said Nina. "I hate that word."

"I think we should leave it in," Detective Williams said. "I bet most homicidal maniacs think of themselves as interesting."

"Interesting has led me down the garden path too many times."

"How about substituting complex for interesting?" Williams suggested.

"Great. That will really ferret out the meshuggeners."

"But that's what we're trying to do here."

"Funny, I never had any trouble doing that before. Now all of a sudden, I have to advertise. . . ."

---

**MARISSA PIESMAN,** co-author of *The Yuppie Handbook,* is the author of *Unorthodox Practices,* the first Nina Fischman mystery, hailed by the *New York Times* as a "snappy caper . . . a hilarious first mystery." Ms. Piesman is a practicing attorney in New York City.

**Books by Marissa Piesman**

Personal Effects
Unorthodox Practices

Published by POCKET BOOKS

# PERSONAL EFFECTS

## A NINA FISCHMAN MYSTERY

# MARISSA PIESMAN

**POCKET BOOKS**

New York    London    Toronto    Sydney    Tokyo    Singapore

This book is a work of fiction. Names, characters, places and incidents are either the product of the author's imagination or are used fictitiously. Any resemblance to actual events or locales or persons, living or dead, is entirely coincidental.

An *Original* Publication of POCKET BOOKS

POCKET BOOKS, a division of Simon & Schuster Inc.
1230 Avenue of the Americas, New York, NY 10020

# PERSONAL EFFECTS

# Chapter
One

"Outliers," said Susan. "Are you familiar with the concept?"

"I don't think so," said Nina.

"You've met a million of them, but you haven't realized that's what they are. Now you have a proper scientific method of categorizing them."

"Enlighten me."

"As soon as I get out of the shower," said Susan as she hung up her towel and stepped into the stall.

Susan Gold and Nina Fischman were in the locker room of their less-than-luxurious gym. They had been best friends in high school and had ferociously kept in touch for the past twenty years, despite living on different coasts or continents. But now that Susan had finally moved back to New York, they seemed to have what had turned out to be mostly a gym relationship. Even though they rarely saw each other in street clothes, they both went often enough to remain close.

Nina put her earrings on. Or in, actually. Nina and Susan had accompanied each other on an ear piercing mission in tenth grade and had shared an earring collection all through high school—until the time Susan had lost an expensive Mexican silver one right before graduation, and the friends, after protracted discussions, had decided to get what amounted to an earring divorce.

Nina sat down on a bench to wait for Susan. She was used to waiting for Susan. She'd been doing it for twenty years. On street corners, in coffee shops, in the Metropolitan Museum of Art gift shop, in front of many now-defunct movie revival houses, at the back of the Bronx High School of Science cafeteria. And, at this moment, on a bench in a somewhat seedy, though reasonably priced, aerobics studio on the Upper West Side.

Susan emerged from the shower and Nina watched as she dried herself off. It was amazing how little Susan's body had changed since high school. It was still basically a pre-adolescent body, long and thin with only a hint of breasts and a waist. Nina, on the other hand, had spent her life watching things pop out on herself and then slowly succumb to gravity's inevitable tug. It seemed more complicated to be Nina, with underwire bras and talcum powder in the summer where body parts rubbed together. Susan's body parts never seemed to touch. Susan was a string bean. Nina was a pear. Both were preferable, Nina thought, to being a mushroom, which meant having a pigeon-breasted body with no hips and reed-thin legs. Although, those kind of women, if they knew what they were doing, could always pull off wearing big, loose tops and short skirts and high heels.

Nina couldn't go near a short skirt. She had spent so many years not having to worry about short hemlines, and she found it extremely annoying that they had reappeared in such full force. Although she tried not to take it personally.

Susan slicked her legs with baby oil. "An outlier," she said as she massaged the oil in, "is a statistical concept that refers to someone who falls at the extreme end of a bell curve. I learned the term in my statistics course this week. I thought it might be useful."

"Useful in what way?"

"To describe all those men I've wasted my life on. It's more emotionally neutral than abnormal."

"Or nut job or maniac or loser," added Nina.

"I'd watch it if I were you. It's not as if you're generally escorted around town by the young Doctor Kildare." Susan was right. They had both dated more than their share of outliers.

"How is that statistics course? Is it bearable?" Nina had taken statistics as an undergraduate, but had only a hazy recollection. It had been an eleven o'clock class which, back then, meant it was hard to get up for. Of course, these days Nina was up at seven, at the dry cleaners by eight, and ready for calendar call in Housing Court by nine-thirty.

"The course is boring and horrible," said Susan.

"What did you expect?"

"I don't know." Susan was a psychiatric nurse. That was her latest incarnation, anyway. Since college Susan had been a macrobiotic chef, a pukka shell stringer, a samba instructor and a day care administrator. It was during the pukka shell phase that she decided to go to nursing school, so her B.S.N. was from the University of Hawaii. Her latest in a long series of nursing jobs was on a psychiatric ward in a Manhattan hospital. She liked working on the psych ward. She liked it so much that she had gone back

3

to school to get a graduate degree in psychiatric nursing. With a master's she'd be able to start a psychotherapy practice on the side.

Nina wondered whether Susan would actually pull this off. Her friend specialized in abortive attempts. But despite her doubts, Nina was a little jealous. Being a psychotherapist seemed like a luxury to her. Nina was a lawyer who represented the elderly indigent for a federally funded program. All day long she had to listen to people's problems and then actually do something about them: fight with the landlord, call the social security office or the collection agency. Solve them. She wouldn't mind the thought of getting paid to sit in an office to say "how does that make you feel?" and at the end of the session "we'll talk about this some more next week" instead of "I'll run right down to court and get an order to show cause." Besides, psychotherapists got to wear pants on a regular basis. Pants were an easy resolution to the hemline quandary.

Nina was actually a little jealous of anyone who hadn't gone to law school, but especially of Susan, who had selected her career based on the fact that it enabled her to change jurisdictions on a week's notice. For Nina, the bar exam was a ritual that had permanently married her to New York. The thought of taking another bar exam was paralyzing. And over the years, on her birthday, when she got a card and a local native craft from wherever Susan was living at the time, Nina cursed the day she had consented to take the LSAT out of curiosity.

Susan had been back in New York for about a year. She had returned for the express purpose of getting married. Not that she had the groom picked out. But with thirty-five on the horizon, Susan had decided she was tired of dating lunatics. What she wanted was stability. A man in a suit. And New York had more men in suits than anywhere else. What Susan hadn't realized at the time, and what Nina had tried to explain, was that a lunatic can put on a suit just as easily as he can put on a pair of carpenter's overalls or a French bikini.

"I guess I didn't expect these courses to be quite so boring and horrible," Susan said. "They're certainly not honing my skills as a therapist."

"I don't think graduate school is supposed to have any real applicability. It's just torture that you have to go through in order to make sure you don't have to spend the rest of your life working with dumb people."

Susan towel dried her hair, which was only an inch long. Nina's theory was that you needed an inch of hair for each inch by which your hips exceeded thirty-four. She kept her own in good supply, of course, though it was annoying in the gym and on unairconditioned subway cars in the summer. Nina picked lint off of her long black skirt as she watched her friend dress. Susan pulled on an oversized red sweater and black Lycra tights. No pants. She was the kind of person who didn't need to wear pants. "Where are you headed?" Nina asked her.

Susan pulled her makeup bag out of her large Guatemalan tote. "I'm exhausted, but I have a cello player at eight-thirty," she sighed and attacked her eyebrows with a tiny comb. One of Susan's prominent features was a pair of dramatic black eyebrows that she spent a good deal of time emphasizing. Of course, these were the same eyebrows that she had spent so many years tweezing into oblivion. Combing was less barbaric than tweezing. Societal eyebrow acceptance had been Brooke Shields' major cultural contribution.

"A cello player? I thought you were looking for a man in a suit."

"He's an *employed* cello player. With the Philharmonic."

"A man in black tie. I guess that counts as a suit. Where did you dig this one up? Through an ad?" Susan met men in all sorts of ways: through fix-ups, her hiking club, crossing the street. She tended to favor personal ads, however. It was more efficient. Sorting through a stack of letters at home was like going on a blind date without actually having to put up with the other person. And she was generous with her rejects, urging Nina to call any she found interesting. But Nina was reluctant. Since Susan described herself as a Susan Sarandon lookalike, Nina felt it would be in the nature of a consumer fraud.

"Yeah, through an ad. Not mine, though—his. I answered it, even though I think there's a strong possibility he might be married."

"Have you met him yet?"

"No, this is only round one."

"Well, good luck. I, for one, am heading home." It was a luxury Nina was allowing herself a lot lately. She'd had a bad time in the romance department this year and seemed to have sent herself to the bench. Of course, every now and then she'd find herself talking to some man and suddenly she'd be flirting uncontrollably, imagining him on top of her, pumping away. But most of the time she was happy to be heading home, with nothing more demanding on her agenda than washing pantyhose. Susan was still on her eyebrows. There was no point in waiting for her. Nina picked up her purse, her gym bag, her briefcase, and her Duane Reade shopping bag. She arranged her parcels so that they were well balanced and slowly went down the stairs to street level.

# Chapter
# Two

I'm late," Susan said.

"You're always late," Nina told her, with a mix of twenty-years'-worth of fondness and resentment. "What are you late for now?"

Nina was rather late herself, having been stuck in the office on a therapy night when the phone rang. It was Susan, and the thought of having to spring for a cab in order to make her seven o'clock session was putting Nina in a bad mood. She tended to spend her money on the experiential, as opposed to the material, but cab rides were not the kind of experiences she enjoyed paying for. A week at Tassajara, a subscription to the Circle in the Square repertory theater, a plate of calamari at Dominic's—that was more like it. And therapy, of course. The ultimate experience.

There was also a category of items that were harder to classify, like Madison Avenue haircuts. Were those experiential or material? Both or neither. Whatever, Nina had an easier time paying top dollar for a haircut than buying six-dollar pantyhose or matching towels or a pair of Vuarnet sunglasses.

"I'm not late *for* anything," Susan said. "I'm *late*. You know, my period is late."

Nina had had this conversation with Susan before. She knew it meant that a cab ride was pretty much a certainty. You couldn't justify abandoning your potentially pregnant oldest friend in the world just to have six bucks. On the other hand, Susan's menstrual cycle generally displayed the same erratic tendencies as her internal clock—the internal clock which led her to show up at various meeting places as if she were living somewhere between the Central and Rocky Mountain time zones. So chances were that this conversation would be moot within the next seventy-two hours, and Nina would be out the six dollars for no reason. She'd have to chalk it up to goodwill.

"How late?" Nina asked, checking her wallet to see if she had enough cash for a cab. She found a ten and leaned back in her desk chair, settling into the familiarity of the conversation.

"Three days." Three days was well below Susan's cycle's usual margin of error. She usually didn't get panicky until she was at least a week late. There must be some reason that Susan was pushing herself into anxiety. For anxiety wasn't something that descended out of the clear blue sky. Nina understood that. There was usually some other element, mixed in with the anxiety, that pulled you over the cliff.

There were two types of anxiety, really. The really awful unmitigated kind, the kind that could really get you into trouble, that you had to beat back with a stick—that foreshadowed hyperventilation and heart palpitations. That kind was rare. Sometimes you felt it in the shower on the day before your birthday or once in a while stuck in traffic in the Lincoln Tunnel.

Then there was the other kind, the kind that gave off a whiff of pleasure, or at least interest. You knew that if you let yourself plunge a bit, there would be something really interesting to obsess about, that although you wouldn't actually be enjoying yourself, you'd be stimulated. Your nose would be twitching like a rabbit's and you'd be as wide-eyed as an owl at midnight. And your hand would automatically reach for the phone and you'd dial a familiar number and off you'd be—examining everything from twenty-seven different angles and starting every sentence with *but*.

And if you were lucky, whoever you had called had their office door closed, or their television remote control clicker nearby, and could settle in and feed you straight lines like "do you really think so?" for forty-five minutes.

Tonight Susan was clearly in the mood to obsess about motherhood. A period that was three days late was merely an excuse, a conversation piece between close friends. And Nina was a sucker for the topic. Over the years, the two friends had logged in a lot of telephone time on this one.

Nina returned the serve with the usual, intended to determine whether or not this was going to be a serious game. "Three days isn't very long," Nina said. "It doesn't necessarily mean anything. I mean, there have been plenty of times that you've been three days late, haven't there?"

Susan sounded serious. "I know," she said. "But this feels different." Could one tell or not? There seemed to be two schools of thought. Some women claimed that premenstrual symptoms were exactly the same as pregnancy symptoms, since up until menstruation your body really thought it was pregnant, making it impossible to tell the difference. But others said they could tell. Some swore they knew right away, with morning sickness setting in the very next day. Some said that their breasts got sore on the twenty-first day of their cycle, instead of the twenty-fifth, or had blue veins running in them, or they got constipated or started falling asleep after lunch. "I can tell," Susan said with a firmness that let Nina know that she was not getting off the phone so fast.

Nina swivelled in her chair so that she could prop her feet up on her wastebasket and leaned back again. "How can you tell?" she asked, cooperatively.

"Itchy nipples," she said. "You know, I've been there before." They both had. There were fewer women than you'd expect who were virgins when it came to this. And lately, amazing historical things were being revealed: that all up and down the Lower East Side, abortion had been an acceptable convention among Susan's and Nina's grandmothers and great aunts; that those same women who sat stoically upstairs while the male half of the orthodox congregation dovened below, were running off to the back alley abortionists with regularity.

Despite these historical revelations, there was still pain. It was like a healed-over scar on a part of your body that you didn't get to see very much or even think about. But every now and then you would catch sight of it, and the emotions would come flooding back.

"I don't think I could go through it again," Susan said. "Last time was a tough one."

"You could write a magazine article. Abortion after thirty-five."

Nina's attempt to lighten up the conversation failed. "I came really close to not going through with the last one," Susan continued. "When I was younger, I just figured I would wait until everything was right. You know what I mean.''

Nina knew. "Of course I know.''

"The concept of childlessness being a permanent state never occurred to me.''

"To me either," Nina said. But that wasn't exactly true. She had always had alarming flashes, even when she was much younger, that things would go on like this forever.

"But what was I going to do with a kid? And that was when I was still in California, where at least it was socially acceptable.''

"Yeah, in New York there are only two ways to be a single mother. You're either a movie star or on welfare. Only people like Glenn Close can pull it off. Although even she has someone who hangs around sometimes, I think.''

"So if I couldn't do it when I lived in a house with a kumquat tree in the backyard and an alternative Jewish nursery school on the next block, how the hell could I think about doing it while working full time, going to school at night and paying nine hundred a month for an apartment that's too small for me to consider keeping a cat? I mean, if there's no room for the kitty litter, where the hell am I going to put a crib?''

"What's the situation? In terms of paternal participation, I mean.'' Nina tried to ask the question as vaguely and gently as possible.

"Unclear,'' Susan said. "As always.''

Nina couldn't tell if Susan meant unclear as to paternal identity or actual participation. Refraining from indulging in a brisk cross-examination, Nina let the subject drop. What did it really matter, anyway? Unclear was unclear.

"Sometimes I think I should just do it,'' Susan

continued. "But the irrevocability of it is overwhelming." It was like nothing else. Susan had spent her life slipping in and out of careers, relationships, domiciles, even hair colors. Irrevocability was clearly not something she was comfortable with. Nina felt the same way to some extent. She couldn't remember making a truly irrevocable decision since she lost her virginity. "I worry that it wouldn't work out so well," Susan said.

That wasn't what Nina worried about. Working out well was such a long shot that she dared not even consider it. What she worried about was going under. Really losing it. So that instead of just an interesting weekly therapy session, you'd have to move onto the psychopharmacologist, staggering from one responsibility to another, popping anti-anxiety medication. "It's worth it," insisted the single mothers she knew, while they fell asleep at meetings, talked twice as loud and fast as did normal people while they were awake, and always seemed to be cutting their fingers while desperately trying to insure that they and their offspring managed to maintain a steady intake of fresh produce.

"Maybe this will all be moot by tomorrow," Nina said. Susan knew this meant that Nina had to go.

"I doubt it," Susan said crankily. She was not ready to end the conversation. But Nina remained firm. Therapy and court were two things you couldn't be late for.

"Keep me posted," she said, and hung up.

# Chapter
# Three

What do you think?" Susan held an ivory earring up to her ear. It was shaped like a Halloween cat.

"They're great," Nina said.

"Want to try them?"

"I'm looking for something a little more sedate."

"You're a bore."

"Susan, I do spend most of my life in court. The last thing I need is scary monsters hanging from my ears. Practicing law is enough like trick-or-treating already." The friends were at a Saturday schoolyard flea market on the Upper West Side. They were doing what they had been doing, on and off, for twenty years—shopping for earrings. In addition to a gym relationship, Susan and Nina seemed to retain an earring relationship, despite their previous difficulties.

"How is work, by the way?" Susan asked.

"Terrific. I got a new client on intake last week. She needed a will and wanted to leave all her money to her plants."

"So what did you do?"

"Talked her into naming the New York Botanical Gardens as her beneficiary."

"I think you meet more nuts in your office than I do on the ward."

"Probably."

Susan put the ivory cats back. "So you wouldn't recommend that I drop my statistics course and go to law school instead?"

"Are you kidding? Law has the most career dissatisfaction of any profession. The statistics are staggering. There was an article in the *Times* recently about this woman who gives seminars for lawyers who are trying to change careers. She said that most of her students feel that practicing law is like being caught in the middle of a nightmare. You want to wake up, but you need the sleep."

"That's how I feel about working in general."

"Believe me, you'd find the legal profession too confining. You'd have to put away your entire earring collection and wear things like this." Nina pointed to a pair of small gold knots.

"Are you telling me that a person should choose a profession based on their aesthetic? That instead of looking at your LSAT scores, law school admissions officers should examine the contents of your jewelry box?"

"In your case, Susan, they wouldn't even have to look at the contents. They could tell by the box." Susan kept her earring collection in an antique tin with Victorian erotica lacquered on the cover. Nina kept her earring collection in stacking ice cube trays. "Did you get your period, by the way?"

"Oh, that." Susan looked like she was going to cry. "It's moot," she said, twisting her mouth in a way that gave Nina a clue to change the subject.

"How was that cello player you were meeting after the gym that time? Any potential?"

"Cute, but definitely married. Looking to squeeze someone in between afternoon rehearsals. If I had been working nights, I would have considered it, but with my present schedule, it just wouldn't work."

"I thought you were looking for a husband. One of your own, not someone else's."

"I know, but he had this magnificent Central Park West apartment with marble fireplaces."

"Where was his wife?"

"Playing the viola out of town somewhere."

"You're too easily distracted from your marriage mission," Nina said. "I think it might mean something."

"I know. All it takes is a marble fireplace and I'm off in an entirely different direction."

"So I guess you got your period after all, huh?"

Susan turned back to the earring table and murmured "I guess so" over her shoulder. She was clearly not encouraging this particular topic of conversation.

"Let's get some apple cider." Nina made it a point to indulge in autumn rituals, since it was the only season when there was any point to living in the Northeast. They walked past the rug guy and the lady who made velvet hats and stopped in front of the cider table. Nina considered buying a jug of maple syrup or a jar of pear butter, but stopped herself. There was no point in pretending she lived in a large, jolly family that consumed hearty country breakfasts. She lived alone and would probably end up pouring the maple syrup or smearing the pear butter over cold cereal at midnight and feeling guilty. She confined herself to a cup of hot cider.

"I haven't given up hope, you know." Susan stared into her cider. "I am onto something promising."

"Someone you've told me about?"

"No, I haven't mentioned him."

"Why not?"

"I don't know."

"Do you care to discuss it now? Or do you want to go back to talking about earrings?"

Susan half smiled. "I'm going away with him next weekend. That's all I'll say."

"Where?"

"Hiking."

"Oh, a hiker. Not too nerdy?" Susan had always been a hiker, but she complained that the New York men who hiked were nerds. The kind of men that wore the same black eyeglass frames they had in junior high school. That all the non-nerdy men in the city were into the Stairmaster.

"Not at all. Good haircut, good build, good wardrobe."

"No black eyeglass frames?"

"Contact lenses."

"Wait a minute." Nina frowned. "Good haircut, good build, good wardrobe, and contact lenses. Are you sure he's not gay?"

"He's not."

"How can you be sure?"

"Don't worry, I can tell."

That got a laugh out of Nina. "The way you could tell with that Brazilian guy in your samba troupe? Or that illustrator in Taos?"

"Oh, please. That was ages ago." It was getting worse, actually. A lot of men seemed to have decided that they hadn't made such a good choice when it came to sexual preference and were attempting to reorient themselves. It was hard to tell, except that every now and then the layer that had been painted over would suddenly pop out. Homosexual pentimento. Some guy who seemed obsessed with his boring job with some bank would turn out to have an opera subscription, or would suddenly drop five hundred bucks on an antique lamp made of pink Vaseline glass. And you would wonder. Nina didn't come up against this problem too often. She wasn't the kind of woman that gay men were attracted to. But Susan, with her boyish body and devotion to a highly developed aesthetic, had a history of this kind of thing.

"Where did you meet this guy?" Nina asked.

"Let's drop the subject. I don't want to jinx it." Susan threw away her styrofoam cider cup and picked up a big black sweatshirt with Jackson Pollock paint splatters all over it. She held it up to her chest. "What do you think?"

"It's you."

"What about you?"

"It's not me," Nina said. "Too entropic."

"This is a word?"

"You know. Too all-over-the-place."

"What happened to the Nina Fischman I went to high school with? Who used to braid her hair with leather thongs and wear purple tights with red Capezio tap shoes?"

"There's just something about my life these days that demands clipping sedate little pearls to my ears."

"Are you clipping pearls or your wings? All you do these days is go home and try to catch up on back issues of the *New Yorker.*"

"I don't know what to say. Somehow wearing purple and going out with strange men makes me feel too vulnerable lately."

"You're letting yourself get old, Nina. Before your time."

"I guess there are worse things than getting old."

"Like what?" asked Susan.

"I don't know. Not getting old, I guess."

"You know, I'm changing my diagnosis of you. I used to put you at a 300.00. A nice acceptable anxiety neurosis, like everyone else I know. But you're developing this morose edge that I don't like. I'd say that you're slipping into a 300.40 dysthymic disorder."

"What's that?"

"Depression, to put it bluntly."

"Susan, spare me please. I pay someone for this stuff."

"And what does she say?"

Nina wondered. She knew her shrink had to fill out a report twice a year for her insurance company. Was she a 300.00 or a 300.40? Were those the choices in life? If they were, she guessed she'd opt for anxiety. It sounded more upbeat than depression. "I really don't know what her official diagnosis is. Maybe she doesn't have one."

"After seven years? No way."

"Can't you be both anxious and depressed?" Nina asked.

"Now, don't get greedy."

She looked at her friend. Susan was not a stable person. Compared to Susan, Nina usually felt pretty functional. She wondered how she'd feel, however, if Susan got married to this non-nerdy hiker. It was premature to worry about it, of course. But picturing Susan finally resolving what had been, so far, a major issue of both of their lives was enough to make Nina feel herself slipping into dysthymia.

# Chapter
# Four

Thank God they were almost cooled down. Usually, she could easily handle forty minutes of aerobicized arm flinging. It had become such a regular activity in Nina's life that it no longer seemed onerous, like dental flossing or checking her pantyhose for runs. For about three and one-half weeks out of the month, her low-impact aerobics class seemed like no big deal. But during those last few days even the lowest of impacts seemed too jarring.

American forms of exercise seemed to be aging along with the baby boom, which was fine with her. Before Nina hit thirty, everyone jogged, or if they did take aerobics, it was the wild kind, where you jumped madly into the air. She had always found it a bit much. But now, since everyone else seemed to be edging gently over the hill with her, the rage had become this very demure toe-heel stuff where you kept one foot on the floor at all times and put most of your energy into flinging your arms. Nina liked keeping one foot on the floor at all times. She found it comforting. And arm flinging was manageable. She wondered what the next decade would bring. How much more could they wind down? Would they have to do the whole class under water, like her mother's senior citizens' aquatics class?

When the class was over, the students and teacher politely applauded mutually, the way karate classes bow at each other. As Nina headed toward the locker room, the instructor called out to her. "Nina, where's Susan? On vacation?"

"I don't think so," Nina said. "Didn't she come yesterday?"

"Nope, she wasn't here. Maybe she's sick."

It was Tuesday. Susan and Nina tried to show up for three or four classes a week. Nina had missed Monday's class and had assumed Susan had been there. But apparently she hadn't come. And she wasn't there tonight. It was unlike Susan to miss two nights in a row. For one thing, she was too gym-obsessed to stay away for more than one night. And, for another, she usually didn't skip classes without calling Nina and checking in with her.

"I haven't spoken to her since Friday," she told the teacher. "I'll give her a call when I get home."

But by the time Nina got home and checked her answering machine, she knew she didn't have to make the call. "You must call me immediately." It was a message from Nina's mother. "It's about Susan." Ida Fischman's voice was controlled, but had a hysterical undertone.

She dialed her mother's number. Ida picked up right away. "Is it something really bad?" Nina asked.

"The worst imaginable."

"She's dead?"

"Yes. Her brother called me this afternoon. He

thought it would be better than leaving a message on your machine.''

"What happened?''

"I wasn't able to get too many details. I didn't want to push, and Scott was really much too upset to talk. All I know is that she was killed sometime during the weekend. They found her body upstate early this morning.''

Upstate. Susan had said she was going hiking with that guy. The guy she had characterized as promising. Well, promising he clearly was not. It seemed that single women now had more to worry about than date rape. These men were moving on to date murder.

"Is the funeral tomorrow?'' Nina asked. Jews buried their dead ASAP.

"Tomorrow morning,'' Ida said.

Nina could have used some time to figure out what the hell was going on, but she'd have to piece it together at the funeral.

"What time, and where?''

"At ten. Up on the Grand Concourse.'' The first thing that flashed through Nina's mind was that Susan would definitely not have wanted a Bronx funeral. Nina could just hear her. "After all this?'' Susan would rail. "California and Hawaii and Mexico and Greece and Morocco and three different undergraduate schools and six different careers and God knows how many men and how many apartments and how many roommates. For what? To have it all end back in the Bronx?''

It was only after hearing Susan's imaginary voice that Nina realized that her oldest friend was really dead and that she would never hear Susan complain about anything ever again. And that's when she choked up.

"Is there anyone you'd like me to call?'' Ida

offered. "Her brother said he couldn't get a hold of Gwen."

"Forget it. Gwen's in Europe." She wasn't so sure Gwen would have come anyway. Susan and Gwen had so many fallings in and out that Nina couldn't keep track.

"He said he managed to contact someone who worked with her and they promised to let people in the hospital know. Is there anyone else we should notify?"

"I'll think about it. Give me a chance to let this sink in before you put me on the funeral committee."

"Well, it is tomorrow morning." Ida was being persistent. "I'd like to go with you," she added.

"You want to go? Why?"

"Don't forget that I've known Susan for the same twenty years that you have."

"Okay. I guess we'll take the D train," Nina said. Her mother also lived on the Upper West Side, not far from Nina's apartment. Late in life, after decades in Bronx tenements, Ida's housing karma had taken a turn for the better, and she had lucked into a two-bedroom West End Avenue co-op. She had her brother Irving and a quirky Manhattan real estate market to thank for providing her with the only asset she'd ever managed to acquire. And the real estate seemed to have done more for her self-esteem than the endless therapy sessions she still attended.

"We'll take a cab," Ida said sharply.

"All right. Whatever." It wouldn't have occurred to Nina to take a cab up to the Grand Concourse. There was something about taxis and the Bronx that seemed mutually exclusive. But she supposed it could be done. Why not? "I think I want to get off the phone now."

"Okay. I'll call you at eight-thirty tomorrow morn-

ing and we'll arrange where to meet." Ida was forever the schoolteacher, gently nudging her class into
appropriate behavior.

Nina wanted desperately to sleep. She would have
taken a valium, had she had any in the house. But
she wasn't the valium type. She never had the time
or money to be high strung. She rummaged around
in her medicine cabinet. The only thing she could
come up with was Tylenol with codeine, left over
from last year's root canal. She took two, but they
didn't help.

As she lay awake in the dark, trying to block out
the sound of a nearby car alarm, Nina attempted to
sort out the many layers of feelings she was having.
The top layer seemed to be guilt. That was predict-
able. Guilt was almost a knee jerk reaction with her.
She had never been one to transcend her ethnic heri-
tage. Nina thought about all the times she had felt
that Susan was more trouble than she was worth, that
it wouldn't be so terrible if she would just drop off
the face of the earth. All those middle-of-the-night
phone calls, the wiring of money to Morocco, the
abortion that Susan had the year before they became
legal.

And the more subtle stuff, the demands that were
small but disrupted your day—a lost borrowed earring, not enough cash when the bill came, a credit
card that had gone stale. And all that waiting on
street corners that Nina had gone through. That had
recently been replaced by hanging on the line once
Susan got call waiting.

The car alarm finally stopped and Nina was able to
think about the more tender moments. About how
she and Susan were still able to laugh really hysteri-
cally together after all these years. She couldn't really
let go that way with anyone else. Maybe it was some

kind of bonding you had to form in adolescence. And she thought about how they had kept each other posted through all of the phases of their lives so that they could always get each other's jokes, no matter what the frame of reference. And as everyone else in Nina's life seemed to gracefully sweep out of adolescence into marriage, motherhood, and career satisfaction, there would always be Susan, squinting up at the bride, new mother or graduate degree recipient, shaking her head, claiming to still be too young and restless for all that.

Except lately, when Susan had decided that it was time to marry herself off. And look where that had gotten her. Maybe she should have let herself go on the way she was, thought Nina. Susan could have let her bristle cut go gray and turned fifty like Gloria Steinem, explaining to everyone in a droll voice that she didn't breed in captivity.

Well, Nina was sure it was easier to do that when you were Gloria Steinem. Although she also had a strong feeling that old Gloria was probably a 300.00 anxiety neurosis or a 300.40 dysthymic disorder to some shrink somewhere. But one thing was certain: these were not times that made it easy to toss your head at domesticity and convincingly claim to be uninterested in all that. Susan had known that and was tired of trying to pull it off. And Nina had understood. The impulse to just get married already was a strong one. She often felt like doing the same, even if it was only just to move the plot along. But she hadn't been prepared for this. Susan's murder was a plot twist that Nina had never anticipated.

# Chapter
# Five

The morning of Susan's funeral was one of those blue-and-orange October stunners, when the world looks like a huge Mets logo. Nina had to make half a dozen phone calls to find someone to cover for her in housing court that morning. It was funny, she thought, how it used to be that the most important thing in life was knowing that any minute you could split. And now it was more like taking half a day off wasn't worth the hassle. Well, it would be a whole day, actually, since there would be the funeral and then the cemetery and then the shiva, either at Mr. and Mrs. Gold's apartment in the Bronx or Scott's house in New Jersey. Nina generally found sitting shiva helpful. It was one of the few Jewish rituals that worked, unlike fasting or separating milk and meat or men and women.

Funerals were easy to dress for in New York. Nina, like all the other women in Manhattan, had a closet filled with black clothes. So she had a lot of choices. She considered a wrap jersey dress that was an old favorite, but it really would have to be sedated by a pin. She decided instead to go with a suit. Jesus, she finally got a day away from court and she ended up having to wear a suit anyway. Things didn't used to be like that.

Nina was meeting her mother in front of Fairway, the fruit and vegetable palace on Broadway between 74th and 75th. As soon as she got there, she realized it was a stupid place to meet. Probably the most crowded spot in town at this hour, if you didn't count the 72nd Street IRT station. There you had to wait in line just to get on the stairs. On this Wednesday morning, Fairway was teeming with eighty-year-old ladies pushing shopping carts and forty-year-old ladies pushing strollers. And all of them bumping into each other. Fairway was a bad scene if you were prone to Type A behavior. Nina would never attempt to push a cart around in there. Even one of those hand baskets was too cumbersome in the over-crowded aisles. Nina travelled light in Fairway, darting from aisle to aisle, piling her arms with groceries until she couldn't carry any more. You needed guerrilla tactics to survive in a place like that.

As Nina watched a gnarled gnome in a loden coat puzzle over a jicama display, Ida appeared. Nina always found the first glimpse of her mother shocking. On the phone, Ida sounded so self-assured that Nina forgot she was an old lady. But when she actually saw Ida, her immediate thought was 'what's Grandma doing here?' Nina knew that the process was inevitable. It was happening to her also. It was a well-known phenomenon—one day you pull your sweater on and your mother's arm pops out through the sleeve.

Ida was wearing a black cape. She as one of those

mothers who had always worn capes and ponchos and shawls and all sorts of things without sleeves. As if not having sleeves automatically made you more interesting. Having a sleeveless mother would have been all right under the correct circumstances, but it had been pretty mortifying back in the Bronx in 1960, among all those bowling shirts. Now, of course, on an October morning in the fin-de-siècle Upper West Side of Manhattan, her sleeveless Mom looked just fine. Especially since Nina had collected quite a few wraps of her own.

Ida had that proud and determined look shared by all those old ladies who weren't rich but had managed to hang on in Manhattan. A look that just dared you to try and ship them off to Miami or Scottsdale. "How are you doing?" Ida asked Nina, and hugged her.

"I'm okay. I didn't sleep much, though."

As Nina spoke, Ida turned and picked up a cantaloupe from a nearby pile. She gave it a delicate squeeze and then a sniff. "Umm, nice," she said.

"Ma, come on. Put the cantaloupe down. Let's get a cab. We're not showing up at the funeral with a bag of fruit."

"I wasn't shopping, I was just squeezing. You see a bunch of melons, you test one for ripeness. It's human nature."

"You are a fruit pervert, consumed by an uncontrollable urge to fondle."

"My God, since when is it an unnatural act to pick up a cantaloupe?"

"Can we get this show on the road?" Ida put the melon back as Nina stepped off the curb and hailed a taxi. She tried to maintain an air of casualness when hailing cabs. There was nothing worse than a woman who looked hysterical while hailing. These women

27

were always dressed in some expensive outfit, standing on some East Side street corner, looking like they would just die if they didn't get a cab *immediately*. You just knew they were off on some ridiculous mission—like getting their pores tightened—that they considered of drop-dead importance.

So Nina avoided a sense of urgency while hailing, and once inside the cab, she usually tried to adopt a collegial rapport with the driver. As if it were only temporary that he was in the front seat and she was in the back, that they were basically interchangeable, and at any minute they might both get out of the taxi and Nina would slide in behind the wheel and drive *him* someplace. It had been easier to maintain this illusion when she was younger, especially since she did spend one of her college summers actually driving a cab. But now, what with Nina wearing suits and heels and carrying a briefcase, and fewer and fewer cab drivers even speaking English, much less being English lit graduate students with denim jackets and adorable little beards . . . well, the illusion was wearing thin. But Nina still tried to at least smile and be pleasant, even when these guys tried to give her an argument about taking the Queensboro Bridge over to LaGuardia Airport.

The driver that morning was actually Jewish, one of the last of the breed who wore caps and carried cigar boxes. "We're going up to the Bronx," Nina told him. "Go down to 72nd, make a right and get onto the Henry Hudson, going north."

"Lady," he said, "you think I don't know how to get to the Bronx?"

"Are you from the Bronx?" asked Ida, as if encountering a long-lost relative. Her mother's landsman routine used to embarrass Nina, like the sleevelessness. But now, like the sleevelessness, she indulged in too much of it herself to give Ida a hard time about it. "The Bronx" had become two of Nina's favorite words.

She listened to her mother and the driver discuss the past glories of the borough, since it turned out that he had, of course, grown up a mere two blocks north of Tremont Avenue and one block north of Ida. As her mother went on about the old Concourse Plaza hotel and summer evenings in Crotona Park, it was hard for Nina to believe that this was the same childhood that Ida was still, at the age of seventy, whining about in therapy. She was about to point this out, but as the cab turned east onto the Cross Bronx Expressway and Nina caught sight of the old NYU campus and—a little to the south—Yankee Stadium, she started to get a warm, nostalgic glow herself. The sight evoked a time when Mantle and Maris were breaking home run records and the corners had candy stores with bookies and *a cappella* singers hanging out in front of them.

Of course, Nina had been filled with contempt for all this, even at the age of six. But she found herself getting into the mood. There was nothing more heart-warming than a mutually shared session of Bronxophilia. As Ida and the cab driver reminisced about James Monroe High School, Nina joined in with anecdotes about Krum's ice cream parlor and hanging out on the Pelham Parkway wall. By the time the cab reached the Grand Concourse, the driver never would have believed that these two women had spent their entire lives scheming to get the hell out of the Bronx.

# Chapter
## Six

The funeral parlor dated back to the days when mosaic ashtrays and walnut veneer were in fashion. The predominant colors were turquoise and orange. Apparently periodic redecorating was not mandatory in the funeral business.

Jewish funerals typically had four acts. The first two acts took place at the funeral parlor. Act One was sort of like drinks before dinner, with all the mourners wandering around a room filled with living room furniture, kissing each other hello and telling each other that next time they hoped to meet on a happier occasion. Act Two was the ceremony, which took place in a chapel equipped with pews. Act Three took place at the cemetery, where a prayer was said over the body, and the immediate family got to shovel some dirt onto the casket. Not the entire immediate family, actually, just the men. The final act consisted of sitting shiva, which stretched out over a week. After the cemetery, the mourners would go back to the home of the spouse or child of the deceased, except in circumstances like this, where there was no spouse or child. One more reason to get married, Nina thought. It's very uncool to have people sit shiva at your mother's house.

Nina and Ida wandered into the middle of Act One. The crowd was a familiar one. Not that Nina actually knew any of these people, but she had been to enough family funerals to know that there was usually a stock set of characters and the individual players were basically interchangeable. Jewish funerals generally brought out a lot of old people, which made it difficult to go to the bathroom. There was always a long line of old ladies with canes and walkers that had trouble negotiating the toilet stalls.

The crowd here looked a little younger than usual. The first person Nina caught sight of that she actually recognized was Susan's cousin Rhonda. She hadn't seen Rhonda in twenty years, but she recognized her immediately. Rhonda still had the biggest breasts to come out of Queens. The fact that they were draped in black didn't seem to make them look any smaller.

"Rhonda, it's Nina Fischman," she whispered. "Do you remember me?"

"Of course." Rhonda gave Nina's wedding ring finger a quick check as she dabbed at her eyes. "How are you?"

"This is my mother, Ida Fischman. Rhonda Prosky."

"It's Katz now. Rhonda Katz," she said and squeezed Ida's outstretched hand. "Isn't this the most terrible thing you've ever heard of?"

"I really haven't gotten any of the details. I got home late last night and Scott had called my mother to tell her. All I know is that she was . . . you know." Nina's voice trailed off.

"She was found strangled to death on top of a mountain," Rhonda hissed dramatically.

Somehow the phrase "on top of a mountain" sounded ridiculous in the middle of the Bronx. But Susan and her boyfriend had been hiking, and sometimes hiking trails go up mountains. "I just can't believe that this happened," Nina said. "I mean, Susan has gone out with some losers in her life, but I always assumed she would draw the line at a homicidal maniac."

"What do you mean?" Rhonda's eyes got very wide.

"She went upstate on a date last weekend. It stands to reason that whoever she went with must have killed her. Or at least knows something about it, doesn't it?"

"You've solved it. You've solved the murder." Rhonda's voice rose from a dramatic hiss to a scream. She pulled Nina over to Mr. and Mrs. Gold. Susan's parents, who were diminutive under normal circumstances, had crumpled into absolute midgets. They looked disoriented as Rhonda continued to yell "she's solved it, she's solved it." Suddenly a large black man appeared, effectively blocking out the little Golds.

"Miss, if you don't mind?" He gestured her over to the corner of the reception area. "Now, who are you?"

"Nina Fischman. An old high school friend of Susan's."

"Pleased to meet you. I'm James Williams, a detective with the New York City Police Department." They shook hands. He looked around fifty. Not bad looking, though a bit bulky, thought Nina. "We're working in conjunction with the Ulster County Police on Susan Gold's murder." His monotone was calming against the wailing that was going on in the background.

"Officer, I'm a little at sea here. When and where was the body found?"

"She was found strangled in the woods upstate, on Slide Mountain in the southern Catskills. We assume the murder took place on Saturday, although her body didn't turn up until yesterday."

"Did anyone even realize she was missing? I know I didn't think about it until last night."

"No one realized it until the body was found. Luckily she had identification on her. Apparently it wasn't unusual for the victim to miss work on a Monday without calling in. Now, who was that woman and why was she claiming that you knew something about the murder?"

"That was Susan's cousin Rhonda. They always hated each other fiercely. Susan and Rhonda made an art form out of mutual contempt. I don't know what Rhonda's going to do now that Susan's not around to make her look good. But that's not really relevant. I don't think Rhonda knows anything about the murder. They didn't have that much to do with each other lately. But Susan and I were pretty close. Last week she told me she was going hiking on the weekend with some guy she'd recently started dating. Is this the first you've heard about him?"

Williams nodded. "Apparently she doesn't keep her family carefully informed about her activities."

"That's an understatement. Besides, women like Susan and me don't really have that much to do with our families."

Williams looked at Nina for a moment and then glanced over her shoulder. "Is this your mother?" he asked. Nina realized that Ida was standing behind her.

"Oh, Ma, there you are." Nina pulled Ida around to meet the police officer. "This is my mother, Ida Fischman. This is Detective Williams. He's working on Susan's case."

"Pleased to meet you," Ida said.

"Same here."

"I was just telling him," Nina said, "that women like Susan and me don't have that much to do with their families. Would you say that was true?" She turned to Ida.

"Well, yes and no," her mother answered.

"What do you mean, Ma?"

"Well, sometimes you have too much to do with us and sometimes too little."

"You mean, for example, I might not tell you that I was planning on getting married, but I keep a constant running dialogue with you in my head. Something like that?"

"Something like that."

"Do you understand what we mean, Detective?" Nina couldn't tell if he was getting it or not. He looked confused, but he also looked amused. "It doesn't really matter. At any rate, I wouldn't spend a lot of time questioning her parents or her brother. I really don't think it would yield too much information."

"I hear you," Williams said. Behind them a door opened and everyone started filing into the other room.

"I'd like to speak further with both of you after the funeral," he said.

Nina nodded. "Anything we can do to help. Of course, my mother doesn't really know anything. She's just here because . . ." Nina trailed off. "I don't know. Why are you here, Ma?"

"Well, I've known Susan for twenty years. So I felt I should come. Also to give you moral support."

"Really? Moral support? I never think of you that way. But I guess it's true. Maybe what I said about women like us not having that much to do with their families was off base."

"I don't think we have time for this right now," Williams said. "Shall we?" He motioned them forward.

Nina and Ida walked in with Williams between them. He seemed to be the only black person in attendance, and they attracted a lot of attention. It was a cheap thrill, Nina admitted to herself, to walk into a roomful of grieving orthodox Jews in the Bronx and pretend that you had married interracially. It was a cheap thrill, but she'd take it. Cheap thrills these days were rare. You took them when you could find them. She almost found herself taking Williams' arm as they slid into a back pew.

The casket remained closed, as it did at all Jewish funerals. It was plain pine and covered with a cloth. The more Orthodox Jews, despite having a predilection towards putting chandeliers in their bathrooms, stuck to unadorned pine boxes.

"I thought men and women sat separately," Williams whispered.

"Only in temple," Nina said.

"That's not strictly true," Ida added. "I've been to some very Orthodox funerals where the men sat on one side and the women sat on another."

"Really?" Nina said. "I didn't know that."

"I think the service is beginning," Williams said.

"All right, we'll shut up." The Fischman women settled back into their pew.

The rabbi walked up to the podium and cleared his throat. He was extremely old. He looked the way a rabbi should look, not like in the suburbs, where they had rabbis that looked like opticians. This guy could not have been anything else but a rabbi. And his voice was a rabbi's voice. A voice that would have been useless selling eyeglasses but was great for burying people.

It seemed that the rabbi had been hanging around the Gold family for a while, because he started the eulogy by discussing how many of Susan's relatives he had buried. Sort of establishing his credentials. Susan's grandmother had been a fine example of Jewish womanhood. Her Aunt Mildred was an extremely spiritual person. Her Great-uncle Hymie was a source of pride to his community. "Cut to the chase," Nina whispered to her mother.

"What else do you want him to talk about?" Ida whispered back. "He obviously has had no recent contact with her. Correct me if I'm wrong, but I'll bet Susan hadn't gone near a rabbi in decades."

"Wrong. She had an affair with some New Age rabbi in the Bay Area a couple of years ago. So there. And when's the last time you went near a rabbi, big shot?" She poked her mother in the ribs.

"It just so happens that my professor of twentieth century European history is also a rabbi."

"You mean that old guy you have a crush on at the New School? That doesn't count."

"Well, neither does running around Berkeley with some born-again Jewish guru." Williams bent slightly in their direction, clearly listening.

The rabbi had finally finished setting forth his curricula vitae as to various Golds and was getting around to Susan. "This little girl," he said, "has been taken from us at a time when it was least expected." Jesus Christ, thought Nina, Susan would have hated being called a little girl by this guy. Nina half expected her to rise up from the coffin and take a shot at him. But the lid stayed shut and he continued. "This little girl was never given the opportunity of creating a Jewish home, of lighting Shabbos candles with her daughters. She will never know the joy of having a child confirmed, as her own mother did. And how well I remember her brother Scott's bar mitzvah.'' The rabbi spent the next five minutes describing this joyous event at the Pelham Parkway Jewish Center. Susan, being a daughter, had been spared the torment of thrice-weekly Hebrew lessons. But she had also been spared the privilege of enough bar mitzvah bonds to send her through her first year of dental school. The Fischmans, unlike the Golds, had never bothered with such things. Not only hadn't they believed in Hebrew school and bar mitzvahs, but even Sweet Sixteens had been viewed as inherently reactionary.

As the rabbi droned on, Nina thought how he was really onto something. Neither she nor Susan had ever really had the opportunity to create the kind of home where you shared the lighting of Shabbos candles with your daughters, because their entire lives had been devoted to leaving things like that behind, to transcending, which had been their favorite verb for a decade and a half. In Nina's case, she had simply been carrying on her parents' progressive tradition. Susan, on the other hand, had been created to rebel against those two tiny, sobbing people that she had somehow been born to. Could either Susan or Nina have abruptly turned on her heel and become a Friday night candle lighter? Well, Susan had tried to some extent, returning to New York and dating men in suits. And look where it had gotten her. But Nina had gone with the flow and look where it had gotten *her:* Thirty-five, alone, and confused. But at least she was the one wriggling with confusion in the pew and not the one at rest in the coffin.

The rabbi was still referring to Susan as ''this little

girl." Clearly his only recollection of her was as the bar mitzvah boy's little sister. He never actually got around to her post-puberty years. He went straight into "but God must have a plan." Anyone who wandered into the funeral uninformed would have thought that the rabbi was burying a sixth-grader.

When it was finally over, Ida slipped off to line up a ride to the cemetery. Nina turned to Williams, who was staying behind to interview some of Susan's work colleagues who were not going to the cemetery. "Why did you decide to come today?" she asked him.

"It's the obvious place to start my investigation. The Ulster County police are trying to find someone who might have seen Susan up there on the day she was killed. I thought I'd start looking into her life in New York City."

"To see if you could bump into an old high school friend or someone who could give you some clues."

"Right."

"Well, unfortunately, I don't know much about this guy that Susan went out with last weekend. She didn't tell me his name or where he lived or anything specific. Just that he looked good, dressed well, and liked to hike—which rules out a lot of men, actually."

"What do you mean?"

"Most men who like to hike aren't exactly the *GQ* type. I think they prefer hiking because it gives them an excuse to wear flannel shirts and their old BVD tee shirts from college."

"Did she tell you anything else about him?"

"Let's see." Nina tried to replay the conversation in her head, but she seemed to be getting it mixed up with about a thousand other conversations she and Susan had had about men over the years. "Wait, I remember something. She said he wore contact

38

lenses. So that rules out anyone who wears glasses, right?''

"Wrong. It rules out anyone with perfect vision."

"Oh. Of course. People with contact lenses all have glasses, don't they? Especially lately, since eyeglasses seem to have become the new fashion accessory. It's very cool to have Giorgio Armani frames and look like a professor of literature at an English university."

"These are things I'm not up on. But I'm glad that you'll be available to offer assistance."

"The only other thing that Susan said about him was that he wasn't gay. But Susan's perceptions about who's gay and who's not is basically useless." Nina paused. "Was," she said. "Was basically useless."

"I take it she had her share of trouble in the man department?"

"Detective, when you're talking about a thirty-five-year-old woman who's never been married, you're bound to find that she's had her share of trouble in the man department. Unless she's been in a convent since high school."

"What about you? Ever been married?"

"No."

"Ever been in a convent?"

"Can't you spot a Jew when you see one? What's the matter, you from out of town or something?"

"Can't you spot a New Yorker when you see one?"

"All right, we're even."

"Did Susan mention to you what this guy did for a living?"

"No, but I would venture to say that he was employed. Susan was trying to turn over a new leaf, you see. No more bums."

"Well, that wouldn't rule out too many men."

"I don't think Susan would have agreed with you."

"Who else should I talk to? Anyone here besides the people from work?"

Nina looked around the funeral parlor. "Forget about her family. They're the last people Susan ever told anything to. And I don't really know how helpful the hospital people will be. I think she tried to maintain a pretty straight persona at work."

"Isn't there anybody else?"

"Our friend Gwen, but she's in Europe."

"That's it?"

"You know, Susan hadn't been back in New York for that long. And she had been so preoccupied with finding a husband, that she hadn't really cultivated any close friendships. Except ours, I guess. But *cultivate* would be the wrong word. Our relationship didn't really take any energy. We had so much history together, that it was really self-sustaining."

"Okay. Even though it might not lead anywhere, I'd like to interview a few more relatives." He pulled out a business card and handed it to Nina. "I'll be in touch with you shortly. In the meantime, if you think of anything, call."

"Certainly." He turned to go. "Detective? You really should talk to Gwen as soon as she gets back."

"How come?"

"Well, I'm not really sure Susan and Gwen were on speaking terms. They sort of fell in and out and I couldn't always keep track. But when they did speak, Susan told her a lot. Especially about men."

Williams nodded. "I'll talk to Gwen."

Ida reappeared. "I got us a ride to the cemetery and also a ride to the Golds' apartment," she said proudly. Getting rides was a necessary element of a successful funeral in New York City. Funerals and suburban weddings were the only times you really needed a car.

Nina scribbled her home phone number on the back of her business card. "I'll speak to you soon," she said as she handed it to him.

"Ladies, it's been a pleasure." Williams bowed slightly and took off in the direction of the nurses.

"He thinks we're nuts," Nina said.

"What makes you say that?"

"Believe me, Ma. I've been on enough dates to tell when someone thinks I'm nuts."

"I see. Well, let's see if we can find Ethel and Harry."

"Who are Ethel and Harry?"

"Ethel and Harry Lapidus. They're neighbors of the Golds who are giving us a ride to the cemetery. Ethel Lapidus is also a friend of my cousin Henrietta. I recognized her immediately."

"You can really work a crowd. I'll never be able to live up to any of the standards you've set for me."

"So far you're doing okay," Ida said and steered her over to Mr. and Mrs. Lapidus.

# Chapter
# Seven

It probably hadn't been such a good idea to go to aerobics class that night after all. Nina thought that it would be a release, after the funeral and then Harry Lapidus getting hopelessly lost trying to get from the cemetery in Queens to the Golds' Bronx apartment for the shiva.

Sitting shiva had not been a particularly cathartic experience for Nina. For one thing, like the funeral, it seemed to have nothing to do with Susan. The Golds no longer lived in the apartment that Susan had grown up in. After she and her brother Scott had safely graduated from college, Mr. and Mrs. Gold had moved into a brand-new smaller apartment in a Mitchell Lama high-rise with a terrace. Things then hadn't been like they were today, with college graduates facing huge housing costs and flocking back to the nest to save money. The boomerang generation, the media was calling these twenty-three-year-olds that were living again with their baseball pennants and stuffed animal collections.

It never would have occurred to Nina or Susan to move back home. Even college vacations had seemed interminable. Back then it had been easy to just drift into a huge rent-controlled apartment on the Upper West Side and split the three-hundred-dollar rent with four other people. Or stay on in whatever college town you found yourself in, work part-time in a health food restaurant, move into a drafty old Victorian house off campus and add your name to the work wheel. If all else failed, there was always fruit picking on an Israeli kibbutz, olive picking on Crete, or pukka picking on Maui. Between the two of them, Nina and Susan had done all of the above.

So all traces of their daughter had been wiped from the Golds' extremely tidy, extremely decorated French provincial one-bedroom apartment. The photographs of Susan that were displayed on the piano no one ever played also failed to convey a sense of who she had been. Susan in a cap and gown or dressed up for High Holiday services ten years ago was not the Susan that meant anything to Nina. And the conversations Nina had to listen to that afternoon as she drank coffee and ate honey cake were similarly irrelevant. "She was such a pretty girl," said an aunt wearing a platinum blonde French twist and a polyester pantsuit. "So thin." And then Mr. Gold actually dragged out Susan's high school report cards and showed them around. Scott, meanwhile, was very busy playing the married, responsible sibling. While Susan had been busy globetrotting, he had been turning himself into a remarkable facsimile of a fifty-five-year-old periodontist. The whole thing was enough to make you want to toss your honey cake.

So as soon as she hit Manhattan, Nina went running straight for the gym. But once she got there, the place gave her the creeps. The locker room seemed strangely quiet. The Board of Health had once again closed down the sauna. And as the other women put on their combinations of tights, leotards, and assorted shmattes, Nina wondered if they knew. They looked like they knew, but how could they?

Nina pushed herself through the class, concentrating on thrusting and lunging extra hard, but she looked like a looming monster to herself in the mirrored front wall of the classroom. As soon as the cool-down period was over, she stopped on her way to the locker room to rehydrate. The instructor followed her and cornered her at the water fountain. "I heard," she said to Nina. "But I didn't want to upset the class by saying anything."

"How did you hear?"

"It was in the *Post*. With a picture."

"Jesus, I haven't seen a paper all day. I was too busy running to the Bronx and then to Queens and then back to the Bronx—for the funeral and to sit shiva. Do you have a copy, by any chance?"

"Sure." The teacher went over to pick up her huge Sportsac and fished around until she dug out that afternoon's edition. She flipped to page five. "West Side Nurse Found Slain Upstate" the headline ran. Above it was one of the photographs that sat on the Golds' piano. So the rest of the city would remember Susan as her parents chose to—twenty-five years old and all dressed up in Laura Ashley, ready to go to temple. It was probably the last time Susan had let a small floral print come into contact with her body. "You can keep it," the teacher said, handing Nina the paper.

"This place seems strange to me without her,"

44

Nina said. "I wonder if it will ever feel normal again. Maybe I should change gyms."

"It might be a good idea."

Nina was hurt. She had expected the teacher to say don't be silly, it's just a matter of time. Finding an aerobics teacher that suited you was as hard as finding a good therapist. It was very similar, actually. You were trusting your body instead of your mind— both problem areas, Nina noted. "Well, I'll see," she said. "This might not be the time for me to make any drastic changes."

"You're probably right. So does anyone have any idea who could have done this?"

"She had gone hiking with some guy last weekend, but no one seems to know who he was."

"Was it the cello player?"

"Jesus, did you know about him?" Had Susan's life been a soap opera that people used to tune in to daily?

"Well, in the gym, you know how it is. All these women discharging all this tension. They tend to talk rather intimately sometimes."

"So do you have any idea who she went out with last weekend? Since you seem to have been something of a therapist substitute for her." Nina realized she had started sounding snotty, as if she were jealous that Susan had been so promiscuous with her secrets.

"Not that I recall. The last one she mentioned was that cello player."

"Well, maybe I should tell that police detective to interview you." She still sounded snotty.

"Fine," the teacher said neutrally.

Nina felt a flicker of anger. One thing she didn't want to do was start hating her aerobics teacher. With a therapist, you could work out the complicated emotions on the couch. But on the gym floor it was best to keep it simple. The woman was just trying to be helpful, for Chrissakes. Well, Nina supposed that most people hated their aerobics teachers on some level. It was hard to watch anyone glide through anything in life effortlessly. Especially if you were grunting along after them.

When Nina got home, the blinking light on her answering machine was going wild. She really wasn't in the mood. But it gave her an idea. She wondered if the police had checked Susan's answering machine. These things could reveal a lot. Sort of the modern equivalent of a girl's diary. An old message from the murderer might still be on her tape. Nina felt exhausted, but also overstimulated. The way she used to feel in college after smoking dope and staying up all night to discuss the Bhagavad-Gita. She grabbed a jacket, ran over to Susan's building, and let herself in with the extra set of keys she kept for plant watering whenever Susan went out of town. She found Williams there, seated at Susan's desk.

"You're working a long day, aren't you?" she said to him.

"You should have checked with me before you came over here," he said.

"Why? The apartment isn't sealed or anything. It's not technically a crime scene, is it?"

"No, but I'd rather any private investigation you conduct be in conjunction with me."

"Afraid I'm going to fuck something up?"

"Yes, I am," he said calmly, with no hint of hostility. "What are you doing here anyway?"

"I had an idea. I thought I'd check the tape on Susan's answering machine to see if it yielded any clues."

46

"That's exactly the kind of thing I'm worried about."

"I would have fast-forwarded it again so that the messages wouldn't get erased." Nina tried to sound reassuring without being defensive.

"Well, it's already been done."

"Did you find anything helpful?"

"Not really. There were a couple of messages from her mother, followed by the last five minutes of a conversation she had with you. You know, one of those times when you pick up after the machine clicks in and you forget to hit the pause button and everything gets recorded. Unfortunately, the machine must have taped the two of you over all the old messages. But I found the conversation interesting. It gave me some insight into the victim. These things are important." He was working hard to keep a smile off his face.

Nina blushed hard. She flopped onto Susan's futon couch behind him so that he wouldn't see. "Which conversation was this?" she asked.

He swivelled in Susan's desk chair to face her. "I think the basic theme was androgyny in men: when it's attractive and when it's repellent."

"Oh, yeah. I remember that conversation. It must have been about a month ago. But it's a theme that Susan and I have been discussing on and off for decades. Since the year we developed our Mick Jagger obsession."

"It was a mutual obsession?"

"Definitely."

"Did you generally share taste in men?"

"To a degree."

"What about the men themselves?"

"What do you mean?"

"Did you share them?"

"Never. It was like an incest taboo."

"Do you know how Susan met this guy?"

"No. It could have been any number of ways. She ran personal ads in *New York Magazine* as well as answered them. She sometimes went hiking with a group on weekends and occasionally went out with one of the hikers. But Susan was also known to pick up men on her hospital ward and on street corners. She spent all of last April dating a man who had pulled her out of the path of an oncoming taxi. So she could have found this guy anywhere."

"Where did the majority of them come from?"

"Ads, I guess. Besides, this guy was a hiker and Susan use to advertise for outdoor types. So he could have come from an ad. But he also could have come from her hiking group."

"I see."

She remembered an afternoon months ago when she and Susan had sat around, sifting through a pile of responses. They had had a hilarious time, although it had been an afternoon of rather black humor. Nina had come very close to calling some of the men herself, but in the end had chickened out. But now it gave her an idea. "I have a thought," Nina said. "But I don't know if you'll go for it."

"What's that?" Williams shifted his bulk and leaned forward towards her. She noted that he moved gracefully for a big guy.

"You could use me as bait. We could reconstruct Susan's manhunt, running ads and sending me off hiking, and maybe we'd find the guy. After all, we did often find ourselves attracted to the same men."

"You mean use you as Susan's decoy."

Nina pictured a wooden duck with her own head attached to it, hidden among swampy reeds. Sud-

48

denly it seemed too creepy. "Ah, forget it," she said. "It won't work."

"Why not?"

"Well, it's true that Susan and I shared taste in men. To a degree, anyway. But that doesn't mean that the same ones were attracted to us. We were very different physical types, for starters. I assume you've seen pictures of Susan?"

"I've seen Susan."

"Oh." Nina had been spared seeing the body. Jews were into closed caskets. "I don't know what she looked like after this guy got through with her, but when she was alive she was sort of my opposite: long-legged, short-waisted, flat-chested. Dark hair, brown eyes, large generous features. Very Semitic. I have more of the Polish dumpling look. Minus the upturned nose, of course. And she dressed much more dramatically than I do."

"I'm sure all this is true. But it's surface stuff. Underneath, I get the feeling you were very similar."

"In what way?"

"After twenty years of wandering, look where you both ended up. Living a few blocks away from each other, going to the same gym, both in helping professions."

"Both old maids."

"Well, both still dating. Let's put it that way."

"Yes, let's put it that way. Although I have given up dating."

"Since when?"

"Labor Day."

"Okay. Well, I would say, since it's only October, that the jury isn't exactly in on that one yet. Anyway, even in terms of style, you may think of your differences as enormous. But from where I'm sitting, I see two of you as exhibiting a very parallel brand of yuppie bohemianism. The kind of women who used to carry Fred Braun pocketbooks in high school. And wear Capezio shoes.''

My God, she had forgotten about Fred Braun pocketbooks. She hadn't thought about them in years. Yet they had played such an important role in her life back then. Lusting after them, discussing them to death with Susan. The words seemed strange coming out of the mouth of a black cop in his fifties. But he was dead right, of course. About the shoes too. ''And how is it that you can toss these terms about with such familiarity?''

''I used to have a wife who was very big on integrating things. As a result, my daughters ended up spending a lot of time with white kids. High School of Music and Art, Oberlin College, progressive summer camps, places like that. So I was exposed to the cultural advantages that go with such institutions—like Fred Braun pocketbooks.''

''What happened to the wife?''

''She finally married a Jew.''

''And the daughters?''

''One married a Jew, one's a lesbian. They're both lawyers and they live in the Bay Area. The wife lives there too.''

Nina tried to picture his ex-wife: glasses, short hair, and a jaw set with fierce determination. She found even the thought of her intimidating. Sometimes Nina felt that if she could be anything in life— thin, rich, married, famous—she'd choose intimidating. No matter how hard she tried, she couldn't pull it off. And it would come in so handy in Housing Court.

This sudden surprising glimpse into Williams' personal life made Nina feel awkward. She shifted the conversation back to Susan's murder. ''Maybe I shouldn't rule this decoy thing out. It could work, if I were to go about looking for men the exact same way Susan did, round up all the suspects and then, one by one, drag them each up Slide Mountain and see if any of them strangles me. Sounds like fun."

"And if he does?"

"You'll be following right behind. Nothing to worry about."

"Sure." Williams smiled. "Let's do it."

"Wait a minute. When was the last time you hiked to the top of a mountain? Even a little one." Williams looked offended. "Besides, even if you were right behind me, don't you think you'd attract some attention?"

"What's the matter? Haven't hiking trails in New York State been integrated yet?"

"As a matter of fact, they haven't."

"Well, I'll bring my partner as camouflage. He's young, thin, white and heavy into sixty-forty." He used the term casually, as if he'd been shopping for water-repellant fabric his entire life.

Nina was somewhat encouraged. "Okay," she said, "you're on."

"Forget it. I was only playing along with you. I'd never get the department to go for it, even if I thought it would work."

"Why not?"

"Well, for one thing, they'd never allow me to use you as the decoy. Why should they use you when we could use an experienced member of the force?"

"But it wouldn't be the same. It's a subtle thing, this manhunt stuff. Ask any of my friends. Subtle bordering on hopeless. You'd never come up with a policewoman with the same . . . what did you call it? Parallel brand of yuppie bohemianism, I believe it was."

"Don't be so sure. All different kinds of people have been joining the force lately."

Maybe she shouldn't push this. It did seem a little farfetched, not to mention scary. "Should we forget this? I could never screw up my courage to run a personal ad or even answer one under normal circumstances. I don't know if I'd be up for this."

"Giving up so soon?" Williams seemed amused. "I was just about to be convinced."

Now Nina felt a little chicken-shit. Did Williams want her to insist? Did she want to insist? She realized that before she pursued this any further, she wanted to ask her mother.

# Chapter
# Eight

Nina gave the cashier a five-dollar bill. "This is for two adults," she said, feeling guilty. But the cashier didn't even look at her as she handed her a receipt and two green MMA buttons.

"Five dollars?" Ida sounded contemptuous.

"I'm being cheap, aren't I?" said Nina.

"I usually give a quarter."

"Ma, the suggested contribution to the Metropolitan Museum of Art is four-fifty."

"Oh, please." Ida dismissed her with a wave of her hand. "I'm here all the time. My quarters add up." It was true. The Ida Fischman cohort took full use of the city's cultural institutions. Her band of retired schoolteachers roamed from museum to lecture to symphony. The way other mothers spent their lives shopping, Ida Fischman spent her life self-improving. She felt no guilt about giving only a quarter. The city owed her. Thirty years in the public school system, starting in the pre-union days, when she made less than a fairly skilled dishwasher. If she wanted to contribute a mere twenty-five cents to see the latest exhibit of Indonesian textiles, she felt entitled.

"What do you want to see first?" Ida asked.

"Have you seen Velasquez?"

"Yup."

"Canaletto?"

"It hasn't opened yet."

"The costume exhibit?"

"Twice."

"Let's have tea," Nina said.

"You paid five dollars so that two of us could sit down and have tea?"

"We'll walk around later, I promise. First there's something I want to talk to you about." They cut over to the left and meandered through the Egyptian artifacts. Nina always felt a little sad whenever she saw the museum restaurant in its current incarnation. There used to be a big fountain area in the middle. The fountain had been turned into a fancy dining area, with table service and candles. Sleek society matrons and impeccably groomed gay men sat there and tinkled crystal and played with their peas. Surrounding them was an elevated area where retired schoolteachers and their poverty-lawyer daughters drank tea and tried to eat only half of their Danish.

Ida and Nina decided to split a Danish rather than go through the pretense of trying to leave any over. They settled at a table with a good view of the rich people's area. "Ma, I think I'm going to start dating," Nina said as she scrupulously halved the pastry.

"Okay," her mother said. "But if you're just starting to date now, what is it you've been doing for the past two decades? Have you been married without telling me? Do you actually live in a house in Great

Neck with two children, and have you decided to divorce an affluent husband whose existence you've chosen to keep me unaware of?''

"Well, I was sort of tied up with Grant for the past five years. And before that, I wouldn't exactly call those episodes in my life *dates*. Sexual skirmishes might be a more accurate description."

"Whatever. But try to be a little more specific. I still don't understand what you're talking about."

"Remember that police detective we met at Susan's funeral?"

"Of course. Detective Williams. Is it him that you're going to start dating?"

"No, although we're both clear that it would be perfectly acceptable to do so, right?"

"Of course." Ida combined enthusiasm with a long-suffering look. "Perfectly acceptable," she said and added a smile.

"Well, we were discussing using me as bait to catch the murderer. It seems likely that since Susan was on a date with a new boyfriend when she was killed, he's probably the killer. Williams sees Susan and me as the same type. Maybe if I went about looking for a man using the exact same methods Susan did, I might meet the same man. Flush out the culprit. He'll closely supervise, of course, so that we should be able to assume that I won't be murdered in the process. What do you think?"

"How did Susan generally meet men?"

"Personal ads, a hiking group, things like that."

"I think it sounds like a fabulous idea."

"You do? Don't you think it's somewhat dangerous?"

"But think of all the men you'll meet."

That was out of character. Ida was beginning to sound like everyone else's mother. Nina supposed it was only a matter of time. Eventually every mother must feel the urge to recycle her charming free spirit offspring into a baby machine. You had to be firm with these grandmother aspirants. "You already have a married daughter. Not only married, but married to a doctor, with her third child due any minute, and a brownstone and a house in the Hamptons, and a Range Rover."

"I do," Ida admitted.

"Not that she can drive it," Nina added nastily. Laura, Nina's younger sister, had it all, except for a driver's license. "I'm supposed to be the woman warrior, the daughter who refuses to sell herself into the Jewish slave trade."

"Did I say anything about marriage? All I said was that you'd meet a lot of men."

"Implying that you think it's time for me to get married already."

"Look, Nina. I've been a little worried about you lately. You dumped Grant last spring. That was fine. It was probably long overdue. And we both knew that the fling you had with the orthodox district attorney wasn't going to amount to anything. You got out of that without too much damage. Of course, I had high hopes for the federal judge. Who wouldn't? But a reconciliation with an estranged wife isn't something within your control. It happens. However, you seem to have taken that one rather hard. You've withdrawn into yourself. I don't even know what message you have on your answering machine these days. Whenever I call, you're home. It's not like you. You need to snap out of it. This plan sounds very interesting to me."

That was how Ida and Nina judged everything—by whether or not it sounded interesting. Not whether it had inherent social value, or whether it was fun or productive or lucrative, but whether it was interesting. They tried new diets, not because they thought they would lose weight, but because the diets sounded interesting. Ida made her travel plans not on the basis of a good time or reduced probability of dysentery. Nina chose her clients not because of need or likelihood of winning on the merits. They both bought clothing not because it was flattering or a bargain. All these decisions were based on whether or not something seemed interesting. It was also the way Nina chose men. Which was why, at the age of thirty-five, she was still single.

"There's that word again," Nina said.

"What word?"

"Haven't you learned by now? Your antennae should shoot straight up whenever you hear the word 'interesting'."

"I didn't *hear* it. I *said* it."

"Even worse. That's when you're really headed for trouble."

"What's the alternative? Spend your life in pursuit of the terminally boring?"

"Why can't things just be fun for a change? Why does everything have to be so goddamn interesting?"

Ida shot her a strange look. "Nina, I don't want you to be offended by this. Now, I've known you for a long time."

"As long as anyone."

"Right. As a matter of fact, I'm your mother. And I want to say something to you."

"I'm ready, I can take it."

"You never were the fun type. So cut your losses and settle for interesting."

"That's a cruel thing for a mother to say to a child."

"Now, I don't mean that you're not funny." Not being funny was a cardinal sin in the Jewish religion.

"I just mean that you are not one of those carefree fun types. I don't mean it cruelly. You know how much of myself I put into you. For better and worse. And if you're not the fun type, it's probably my fault. But from an extremely early age, you were so busy examining both sides of every issue that you were usually too distracted to have fun."

"It's true. I remember that I never liked to play tag, because I always felt that the act of tagging someone was too unbearably cruel to commit. And, of course, I also felt that if I were tagged, the pain would be too unbearable to survive. And I remember choosing George as my favorite Beatle because he looked the most tortured." The real fun types not only liked Paul the best, but wore "I Love Paul" buttons. Nina never wore an "I Love George" button, because it wouldn't have been politically significant. Nina sighed. Her mother was right. And it was probably too late now to become a fun type. "So you're in favor of this interesting plan?" Nina asked.

"I am. Besides, don't you want to help avenge Susan's murder?"

Yes, of course she did. What was wrong with her, anyway? Her oldest friend had just been killed and here she was, brooding because her mother didn't think she was a fun type. Maybe this was the time to shed her wimpy Clark Kent coat of ambivalence and emerge a superheroine. She could almost see herself as a superheroine, as long as the tights were black and not some hideously unflattering loud color. And thank God they had invented Lycra. It really held you in.

Besides, she had always identified with victims. Here was a chance to turn this neurotic tendency into something useful. In this case, the more she identified with the victim, the greater the likelihood of conducting a successful manhunt. But Nina still felt dubious. "Does it sound plausible to you?" she asked Ida. "Aside from meeting men, I mean. Do you think there's a chance we'll catch this guy?"

"What do I know? I really have no idea how reasonable it is, in a city this size, to expect a murderer to keep turning up like a bad penny. But if Detective Williams thinks it's not too farfetched, then it must be based on something. He looked like he knew what he was talking about."

Ida had the kind of look on her face that meant she had found Williams attractive. It was nice to know that even though your mother was conventional enough to hock you about getting married, she was still open-minded enough to be attracted to a younger black policeman. "Okay," Nina said, "I'll do it. But I just hope you're not encouraging me just because you're the named beneficiary on my life insurance policy."

"Don't be silly." Ida picked up her tray. "Let's go see some art." As they headed upstairs to the Impressionists, Nina couldn't help wondering whether her mother was going to be her named beneficiary forever.

# Chapter
# Nine

SJF or SWF? I wish I could remember which one Susan used to use." Nina handed the legal pad to Williams. "What do you think?" They were in Susan's apartment, after he had gotten official approval, trying to reconstruct one of her personal ads. Williams had carefully gone through each drawer and each pile of paper, but hadn't found any old specimens.

Susan had shown Nina a number of her ads over the years, but they had dissolved into hazy vagueness. As far as Nina could remember, Susan had always stuck to the indoor pleasure and outdoor pursuit form. Comfortable in silk and jeans, hiking and brunching, cross-country skis and limousines. It had been done before. But Susan had maintained that it was a theme that worked well, that New York was filled with women who insisted on taking cabs everywhere, and if you showed an interest in other forms of locomotion, you would increase your results.

Nina and Williams had tried to stick to the formula, but were having trouble coming up with a lead. "Let's not use any of those initials," he said. "They're trite. Think about it. Did she really use that stuff?"

"Maybe not." Nina couldn't exactly remember. He was right, it was trite. How come an almost-retired police detective who lived in a two-family house in St. Albans with his eighty-year-old mother had a better grasp of how to write a personal ad than she did? Maybe she should be worried about this. "And let's take out interesting," she said. "I hate that word."

"I think we should leave it in," Williams said. "It might strike a chord. I bet most homicidal maniacs think of themselves as interesting."

"Interesting has led me down the garden path too many times. Why do I always fall for it?"

"Because you're the kind of person who is easily bored. You've probably been that way since birth. Therefore, you seek out the interesting." He was right again. Williams had answered the question that had dominated thirty thousand dollars' worth of psychotherapy. "Besides," he continued, "are you looking for a husband or a murder suspect? Keep your eyes on the prize."

"My mother thinks I might derive some side benefits from this venture."

"Hope springs eternal."

"You don't think I'll ever get married?"

"Who knows?"

"Just because of that stupid study that said I have a better chance of being shot by a terrorist?"

"Or strangled by a murderer?"

"I'd say *that* statistical possibility has increased dramatically in the past week," Nina said.

"How about substituting complex for interesting?" Williams suggested.

"Great. That will really ferret out the meshuggeners."

"But that's what we're trying to do here."

"Funny, I never had any trouble doing that before. Now, all of a sudden, I have to advertise."

"It's a more efficient method of achieving the true misery you were destined for."

"Not too high an opinion of marriage, huh?"

"I don't know," he said. "I think it's basically an institution that works. Like being middle class. That works too. It keeps your sanity. It's too painful being poor and it's too hard to get rich. So even if you don't feel like you're living the life you were destined for, you stay comfortable."

"Being divorced isn't comfortable?"

"It's okay. But I couldn't have stayed single all those years, stayed on the sidelines while my buddies had kids and bought houses and cars and complained about the cost of college tuition. I wanted to be a player. At this age, though, being single isn't so bad. Most of the talk has switched to prostate problems and bifocals. Those are conversations I can join, married or not."

She didn't know what to say. She was always at a loss when people complained about problems that she had never managed to have. "How about sensitive? Instead of interesting or complex," Nina said.

"Good. But let's use it as an adjective."

"Excellent point," Nina said. "Sensitivity is considered a desirable trait, while being sensitive sounds like you're having a nervous breakdown or something."

Williams scribbled for a while. "How's this?" He sat back. "Let's take a hike," he read. "Professional woman, mid-thirties, attractive and companionable, seeks kindred spirit to share urban pursuits, upstate hikes, and a bit of romance. I'm looking for someone who has found his way in the world, yet has retained enough sensitivity and tranquility to be happy in the woods for a week."

"It's good," Nina said. "I especially like the image of being in the woods for a week. It has that certain psychotic *je ne sais quoi* that we're looking for. Now, what do we do with it?" Nina was trying to sound enthusiastic, but the fun element of all this was eluding her. Think of it as an extremely organized sort of scavenger hunt, she told herself.

"It'll go into the next *New York Magazine*. That's where Susan used to advertise, isn't it?"

"Yeah. Except sometimes she used the *New York Review of Books*. But she said that yielded the wrong kind of man. They had the right kind of politics and education, but they each had some terminal eccentricity that reduced their potential."

"The kind of guys that live in studio apartments crammed with old newspapers and magazines."

"I used to have a boyfriend like that."

"Did you find him through the *New York Review of Books?*"

"No. I told you that I'm a virgin when it comes to personal ads." As soon as she said it, she knew it was a mistake. Too provocative. "Not that I haven't thought about it," she went on. "I mean, you don't get to be my age without thinking about these things. If you're single, that is. But I was sort of tied up in this ambivalent relationship for five years, which reduced the necessity of taking drastic action."

"I know what you mean."

"How long were you married?"

"I'm not talking about my marriage."

"Oh."

He paused and stretched. "I've been involved in an ambivalent relationship for a long time. She's married."

"That must be hard."

"No, as a matter of fact. It suits."

Nina tried to picture Williams' married lover. In her mind she saw a tough Irish lady cop, maybe Williams' partner from the time when he had to drive around in a squad car all day. She would have three kids in Catholic school and an ineffectual alcoholic husband at home. Nina imagined Williams and the lady cop nestled together in the front seat of a squad car, cooping under a highway bridge. Then she pictured a rich wife, dressed in a Natori lounging outfit, entertaining Williams in a Park Avenue duplex, while the husband and kids were off skiing in Gstaad, leaving her home to finish off the Christmas shopping. Nina pictured them sipping wine out of costly crystal as one thin silk strap slipped off of the wife's bony left shoulder. Then her imagination shifted to a trim, energetic black schoolteacher, quietly letting herself into Williams' back door on her way home from her Queens junior high school class. As Williams' large hand encircled her small waist, her math books slipped to the linoleum kitchen floor.

Nina wasn't too familiar with the world of married affairs. Most of her contemporaries had married so recently that there hadn't been any time for affairs yet. And it certainly hadn't been done in her parents' generation. Nina tried to conjure up an image of one of her aunts or uncles locked in deep passion with their spouse's golf partner, but she just couldn't.

Not that she'd claim to never have sat across a restaurant table from a married man, listening to him tell her how funny and interesting and sexy she was— words that you couldn't pry out of a single man with a pair of needle-nosed pliers. If you wanted a man to look at you like you were a delectable little morsel, you had to find someone old and hungry and married. The young, available ones just looked at you in that squinty way, assessing you like a piece of real estate. And that was probably the type of man who was going to answer this ad. She could see it now—a long procession of real estate appraisers, inspecting her for flaws. And maybe one of them was a murderer. God, she hated dating.

"So that's it?" she asked. "We just wait for the responses to come in?"

"Are you kidding? It's hiking season. We don't want to waste weeks waiting." He pulled out a file from a stack on Susan's desk and opened it. "I've gone through her calendar, her bulletin board and the piles of mail that were all over her desk. I've been trying to figure out what kind of organized hikes she used to go on. Now, I have a bi-monthly list of events from a trail conference which lists hikes from various organizations. Susan had checked off several of them. All of the ones that are checked seem to have been sponsored by the Catskill Mountain Club. Does that ring any bells?"

"Let's see. Catskill Mountain Club . . . the CMC. CMC sounds sort of familiar, but I can't be sure."

"Well, we've nothing to lose by trying. What are you doing this Saturday?"

"I have a feeling that I'm going hiking. Is that right?"

"Unless it's a real problem for you."

"I do have a trial scheduled for Monday, but it will probably get adjourned." A trail on Saturday and a trial on Monday. Life was just a madcap whirl.

Nina wondered where her hiking boots were. Probably in the back of her closet somewhere, with her cross-country skis. Relics from the days when she carried a day pack instead of a briefcase. There had been a time when she listened to National Public Radio instead of network television. When she wore big floppy workshirts and saw no need to add shoulder pads. When she took the time to cook whole grains and knit herself sweaters, instead of dropping all of her money at Loehmann's and the take-out sushi place. A time when being a woman and an attorney seemed like something finer and nobler and more inspirational than just nudging a generation forward from bored-housewife to bored-lawyer syndrome.

Nina felt a sudden burst of energetic anticipation. Maybe hitting the trail again was just what she needed. After all, this state of cardiovascular fitness she had attained was going to waste. Why bother running to the gym three times a week if the only other time you got to use all this stamina was when you screamed at people in housing court?

"Okay. And what exactly am I supposed to do on Saturday? Get some man wearing contact lenses alone in the woods and see if he kills me?"

"Not at all. This is really just a test run. Talk to all of the men on the hike an see what develops naturally. Just be yourself. But stick with the group. Don't try to do anything provocative. You're going to be alone, so be sensible."

"You told me when we started all this that you were going to be following behind."

"When you get yourself a hiking date, I'll be following behind."

"You don't have to make my finding a date sound like 'Mission Impossible,' for Chrissakes."

"Don't be silly," Williams said. "I'm sure you can get as many dates as you want." He cast her a sidelong glance. It wasn't exactly like one of those married guys looking at her like she was a delectable little morsel, but it was enough to clearly re-establish that she and Williams were two heterosexuals sitting alone together in a room. And a tiny chemical reaction took place. Nothing explosive, maybe just a solitary atom slipping from one molecule to another. But it was enough to perk her up. These little incidents were needed, especially since most of the men in her life seemed to tell her things more in line with "your client is a blood-sucking parasite."

"So what should I do?"

"Call the trip leader and see if he can arrange for a ride." Williams handed her the flyer. "And then we'll just wait to see what happens next."

She could do that. Waiting to see what happened next was how she lived her life.

# Chapter
# Ten

Nina looked at her feet. They looked like Frankenstein feet. Her hiking boots had swollen them to monstrous proportions. Actually, she thought, it was flattering in a way, since her calves looked almost slim in comparison. She was used to seeing her feet in sheaths of black suede, flat most of the time, slightly elevated for court. Suede was good for women like her. Women who, despite their graduate degrees and international travel, had still not figured out how to polish a shoe.

Looking at her big feet reminded her of her years as an undergraduate, when Nina wore construction worker shoes every day, with reinforced toes and metal rimmed grommets. Her college campus had been muddy. The place had been hastily constructed, with an intention to have it ready for the great waves of the baby boom. Although well-intentioned, New York State hadn't quite pulled it off. They were short on dorm space, so undergraduates were packed in three to a room. And they were behind on landscaping, so what you had was basically five hundred acres of rolling mud. The fifteen thousand students who were packed into the five thousand dorm rooms all wore construction worker shoes. Even the prim little elementary ed majors who had pear-shaped diamonds on their manicured fingers wore clodhoppers on their feet, no matter what the season. Looking at her feet made Nina feel like an undergraduate again, but without the depression that seemed to cling to her throughout her college years like a layer of New York State mud.

Today she was in the back seat of someone's Honda Civic. She had been picked up in front of the New York Coliseum, or what used to be the Coliseum. Now it was slated for demolition. The marquee had been advertising for years now that the New York City Firefighters exam had been cancelled. Every time Nina walked by, she pictured hundreds of hunky, young Irish men lined up in jockey shorts for their physicals. It was an arousing image, for despite the creeping decay and sagging underpinnings of this town, New York City firefighters were still incredibly adorable and sexy.

Nina had been picked up in front of the Coliseum, along with a woman named Roberta, by the driver of the Honda. His name was Mark Kurtz and he was her first suspect. Nina had been given his number by the trip leader. Mark Kurtz lived in Brooklyn and was willing to give rides to Manhattan hikers.

Staring at the back of his head, Nina ran him through her checklist. Susan had described her boyfriend as well dressed and a contact lens wearer. This guy wore jeans, hiking boots, a flannel shirt, a ragg wool sweater and a Woolrich jacket. He was appropriately dressed, but whether that counted as well dressed, Nina wasn't sure. And the contact lens business was equally tricky. He was wearing a pair of aviator sunglasses, not unusual for someone driving on the New York State Thruway. Maybe he was wearing them over his contact lenses. Or maybe they were prescription lenses. Or maybe he had perfect eyesight, which would rule him out. Nina tried to make a determination by shifting her head back and forth behind him while looking through his lenses to see if they distorted the road. She had just about decided that she had detected the slightest hint of distortion when Mark Kurtz glanced into the rearview mirror and made eye contact with her. "Is everything all right back there?" he asked.

Nina stopped her shifting back and forth. "Everything's fine."

"You don't get carsick, do you?"

Actually, she did. Especially in back seats. As a child she was constantly carsick. It wasn't until she got older, and rated a front seat, that the condition subsided. People thought that children eventually outgrew carsickness, but Nina didn't believe it. It was just that they finally stopped getting stuck in the back. "Don't worry. I'll let you know if I feel sick," Nina said.

"If you do, you can switch with Roberta." He clearly didn't want his immaculate little Honda messed up. Could she picture Susan with him? Nina had established through preliminary conversational fits and starts that he lived in Bay Ridge and was employed as a chemist by a New Jersey pharmaceutical company. He seemed very controlled. His car had a brand-new look to it, yet the 1987 parking sticker on the windshield made it clear that it was at least a couple of years old. Mark Kurtz was one of those wholesome, athletic, neat-as-a-pin scientists who bordered on nerdiness.

She couldn't even tell if he was Jewish. Not that Susan had specified, so it wouldn't be worth much as a clue. But the older she got, the more irresistible the urge to play the is-he-or-isn't-he game. It was something that adults always did when she was a child and it used to drive her crazy. At the time it had seemed narrow-minded, parochial, and reactionary. Today she couldn't stop herself. Mark Kurtz could have been a Jewish kid that had gone to Brooklyn Tech and then to Cooper Union. Or he could have been German farm stock and studied chemistry at some midwestern state university and lived in Brooklyn simply because it was an easy commute to New Jersey, from where he had gotten his best job offer. He had no discernible accent, and his looks—tall, bland, and pleasant—offered no clue. And Bay Ridge was a neighborhood that went either way. You had fourth-generation Norwegians and Irish. But you also had disgruntled Jewish yuppies who felt that the rents in Park Slope had climbed too high.

Nina tried to picture Susan and Mark Kurtz waking up in her apartment after a night of passion, Susan's bedroom scattered with antique rayon bathrobes and abalone shells filled with potpourri, her window only half covered with a piece of lace that was too narrow but had been carried all the way home from the flea market in Camdentown. It was an unlikely scenario. This guy seemed too well organized and no-nonsense for Susan. But the tableau had a romantic quality to it, like an American colonel in the Second World War falling in love with a young Parisian whore.

While Nina hummed "The Last Time I Saw Paris"

to herself, Mark Kurtz was describing the day's prospective hike to Roberta. She seemed apprehensive, almost in pain. She was obviously not a seasoned hiker. For one thing, her outfit seemed wrong. She was wearing a three-quarter-length wool car coat. Nina was no expert, but she knew that hiking outerwear was not supposed to come down near your knees and should be made of a fabric invented in this century. It was amazing that the South Pole had been discovered without thinsulate and goretex and polypropelene.

Why was Roberta forcing herself to go hiking, Nina wondered, if it made her so anxious. Was it that she found most other singles events even more painful? Probably. At least with hiking no one expected you to keep up a clever chatter, and there were none of those dreadful periods when you had to scour the room looking desperately for someone to talk to. With hiking it was just forward march. And on the ride up, you just had to sit there. And Mark Kurtz could talk to you or not talk to you, but there was none of this prowling about, looking for the most desirable seating partner. Nina had always thought there was a lot to be said for arranged seating. Carry that one step forward and you had arranged marriages.

She examined the back of Roberta's head. She was a social worker, Nina guessed. Although, these days it was hard to tell. Some of the women you'd swear were social workers turned out to be public sector lawyers. Like Nina. When she was in college, she took a vocational aptitude test and all of her suitable careers turned out to be different kinds of social workers. So she did what all good feminists of the seventies who were born to be social workers did—turned her back on such a traditional women's career and went to law school—and ended up with a job that was eighty percent social work and twenty percent higher salary.

But somehow she couldn't quite picture Roberta in court. Never mind, she told herself. You don't have to scrutinize her. It doesn't matter if she's a social worker or a lawyer or the co-chairman of mergers and acquisitions at Goldman Sachs, for Chrissakes. Concentrate on *him*.

Actually, she wasn't even here to be a sleuth. Technically she was here as bait. Williams had told her to talk to all of the men on the hike and see what developed naturally. To just be herself. It sounded like the advice she used to get from *Seventeen* magazine in junior high school, which had resulted in not one boyfriend. Not even a flirtation, unless you counted Joey LaRosa constantly pulling her chair out from under her every time she tried to sit down. As a result, Nina was wary whenever anyone—be it an editor of a women's magazine or a middle-aged New York City police detective—told her to just be herself and see what developed naturally.

What was developing naturally now was carsickness. And they weren't even off the Thruway yet. It would get worse once they hit Route 17. And then the backroads would finish her off. "Roberta?" Nina ventured. "Would you mind terribly switching seats with me?"

"Oh, not at all," she answered quickly. "Are you feeling very sick? Would you like to stop for a while?" The woman probably was a social worker, not a lawyer. There was something about being a lawyer that changed you, even if you had started out caring and nurturing. Years of constant negotiating had the effect of making you assess everything dispassionately enough to determine its consequences. It was this cold-blooded analytic edge that would prompt, before making such an offer, to check one's watch to see if there was time to stop.

"No," Nina said, "I'll be fine once I get into the front seat." Kurtz pulled the car over and Nina slipped in beside him. As she buckled herself in, she turned her attention to him. "I always think that I've outgrown the carsickness and then I get hit again. When I was a kid all you had to do was say Taconic Parkway to me and I'd get nauseous. I'm still wary of taking the Taconic. That's the thing about staying in the town you grew up in. You have to keep riding the same roads that made you sick as a child."

Kurtz gave her a neutral, examining look, as if he were at work and she were a complex molecule. He did not choose to respond. "What about you?" she continued. "Did you grow up around here?"

"No, I'm from Western Pennsylvania. But my wife was raised in New Jersey and she wanted to be near her family, so we moved here."

Wife. Did that mean she could rule him out? Maybe he had withheld that information from Susan. Or maybe he was making it up to get Nina off his back. She'd have to probe a bit. "Doesn't your wife like to hike? How come she stayed home?"

"Oh, she's a real hiking fanatic. She usually comes, but she had some foot surgery last month, so she'll be out of commission for a while."

Roberta leaned forward. "How's Janet doing, by the way?"

"Better, thanks. But I don't think you'll see her on the trail again until next spring."

"Well, send her my best." So he hadn't made her up. Nor was he in the habit of failing to disclose her existence. She could rule out Mark Kurtz. And she could stop trying to peer through his sunglasses to see whether or not they were prescriptive. So she spent the rest of the ride listening to him describe some new chemical compound he was on the verge of patenting.

# Chapter
# Eleven

The hiking group was scheduled to meet at ten o'clock at Catskill Gate Lodge, a spartan inn and hiking center near several trail heads. They pulled in at about a quarter of ten, and as they walked over to the lodge from the parking lot, Nina could smell wood smoke. It wasn't something she got to do in the city, unless there was a burning tenement nearby. On the porch, in the sun, about a dozen hikers stood, gossiping, sipping hot cider, and adjusting the straps on their day packs. It was a pleasant-looking group, with their gaily colored fair isle sweaters and knit caps, like a scene from the L.L. Bean catalog. Except that they were all women. Women that looked a lot like Roberta. Or like Nina, for that matter. Where were the rugged mountain men, the rock climbers, the expedition experts? This could have been a reunion of her freshman dormitory. There wasn't a suspect in the lot.

Most of the women seemed to know Mark Kurtz,

who introduced Nina around. "Who are we waiting for?" she asked him.

"John's driving up a group. I'm sure he'll be here soon." John was the trip leader Nina had spoken to on the phone, the one that had arranged her ride with Kurtz. He, at least, was definitely male. But was he some kind of Manson character, with a hiking harem of Cookie Rabinowitzes instead of homicidal Squeaky Frommes? Nina pictured Charles Manson pulling up in a battered, old Volkswagen camper and then strangling Susan to death on a deserted trail. By the time the next car pulled up, Nina had mentally turned John into a mass murderer.

But the man who climbed down from the Isuzu Trooper didn't exactly fit Susan's description. He wasn't well dressed, he wasn't well built, he didn't have a good haircut and he certainly didn't wear contact lenses. He was short and scrawny, with a cowlick, and his shirttails crept out from his sweater. And he wore the kind of glasses that were probably provided free by an employee vision care plan—the plastic kind that didn't involve an upcharge. He had a bit of a limp, which didn't seem to slow him down as he crossed over to the porch. Three Cookie Rabinowitzes climbed out of the car and followed him.

"How is everybody?" he asked as he stepped onto the porch. He had a pleasant, booming baritone and a nice, crinkly smile. Nina reconsidered her conclusion to eliminate him from consideration. Maybe his charm was so great that it had exerted a Svengali-like force, convincing Susan that this runty guy was actually an Adonis. It seemed doubtful, but she probably shouldn't dismiss him out of hand.

The hike that day was described as moderate on the map posted in the lodge. Nina's plan was to try to stay up front with John and engage him in conversation about his contact lens experiences. But the little limper was too fast for her. She found herself bringing up the rear with Roberta and one of the women from the Isuzu. She had a sense of failure nipping at her, but she consciously beat it back. The day was too gorgeous and the grade really wasn't steep enough to torture her. Although she wasn't terribly sure-footed and her left boot was giving her the beginning of a blister, the aerobics classes seemed to be paying off. And Roberta and the other women were proving to be good company.

Roberta turned out to be neither a social worker nor a lawyer, but a former librarian who had started her own business. Something about computerized consulting to information service companies. The idea seemed amorphous to Nina, but also clever. And the other woman, whose name was Karen, was a nurse-midwife who kept them entertained with fascinating stories of medical obstetrical ineptitude. Sometimes the company of women seemed to Nina like a big, warm swimming pool that she could stay in for hours. If only that obnoxious little lifeguard of heterosexuality wouldn't always be blowing its whistle and screaming "out of the water." That wasn't entirely true, of course. You stayed in the water long enough and some woman was bound to kick water in your face and make you feel like a piece of shit. Or eventually you would get cold, since you never had made the leap into giving up men entirely. But there were very long stretches when the company of women seemed to be the way it should be.

Her mission today, she told herself, had nothing to do with the lifeguard of heterosexuality. She had an assignment to perform and that didn't require taking anything personally. So when the group reached the crest of the ridge and stopped for lunch, she forced herself to sit down next to John and engage him in conversation.

"Not too hard a hike for you, I hope," he said, as Nina stumbled over a rocky toe trap and sort of fell at his feet. "You seem to be doing just fine."

"I am. I know I've been bringing up the rear, but it doesn't bother me. I'm having a good time." She unzipped her day pack and pulled out a peanut butter sandwich. There was something about hiking and peanut butter that went together.

John was eating trail mix out of a Ziploc bag. "That's the right attitude," he said. "If you can learn to pace yourself, that's the whole game. Anyone can hike any distance, it's just a matter of how long it takes. And if you keep at it, you'll notice your pace getting faster. Or maybe not, but that's okay too. There are plenty of people who've been bringing up the rear for years and have been having a great time doing it. Nothing wrong with that."

"Not your typical New York attitude. The city where if you're not first, you're last. And if you're last, you lose."

"New York's a big city. There are all sorts of folks there. Actually, there's a kind of patience you see in New Yorkers that proves beneficial in hiking. Well, maybe patience is the wrong word. Tolerance is more like it. They're used to adverse conditions, which is helpful on the trail. You get some new hiker who's never done anything but drive on suburban highways and shop in malls and their frustration tolerance is absolute zero. They come hiking once and never come back. Give me a subway rider any time."

Nina looked at him thoughtfully. He had a folksy charm that was compelling. Susan hadn't used to go in for that country rube kind of thing. She had been more drawn to urban ethnics. But one never knew.

"That's interesting," she said. "Why so many women, by the way?"

"Maybe for the same reason."

"You mean we're used to adverse conditions?"

"Right. I actually have a few theories on women and hiking, if you care to hear them."

"Certainly. If you care to share them."

He put away the rest of his trail mix and pulled out an orange, while Nina tried to imagine not finishing anything that had chocolate chips in it. "First of all," he said, "women have become increasingly concerned about fitness lately. Yet most remain resistant to the idea of competitive sports. Let's use you as an example. Do you do any physical activity during the week?"

"I go to aerobics classes."

"Ever play squash?"

"Never."

"Any team sport?"

"Not unless you count women's volleyball in high school. But only because it was mandatory."

"What phys. ed. courses did you take in college?"

"Synchronized swimming and folk dancing."

"Think about it. Isn't hiking the outdoor equivalent of synchronized swimming and folk dancing?"

"I guess so. In a way."

"You see, it's a cooperative venture," he said. "A group gets together and decides where and when they want to hike. Then they all set off with the same destination and look out for each other in the process."

Karen, the nurse-midwife who was sitting nearby eating an apple, broke into the conversation. "You make it sound more like the outdoor equivalent of a quilting bee," she said. "Now I have an entirely different theory on women and hiking. It has less to do with cooperation and more to do with survival."

"Okay," John said. "Let's hear it."

"Thanks for permission to speak." Karen was clearly not a member of whatever harem may or may not have existed. "I think that a substantial percentage of our generation of women is experimenting with surviving on our own. Without husbands or children or elderly female relatives clucking over us. With only a few well-chosen friends, and those kept at a distance. The idea of having limited support systems is exciting in a way, but also terrifying. You need to be sure that you really have developed your own survival skills. And hiking proves to you that you have. It's just you, bashing your way through the elements for two hours or two weeks or whatever. And you prevail, thereby coming away having proven to yourself that you are capable of survival in its purest form. For me, it doesn't matter if I'm with a group or not."

"But you have to admit," John said, "that you're very unusual in your predisposition to hike by yourself."

"I don't hike by myself. I hike with my dog."

Nina looked at Karen. She was small and delicately built, but there was nothing fragile about her. She looked pretty fierce. One of those women that made Nina feel like a marshmallow, who owned a four-wheel-drive vehicle and laughed at Nina's discomfort with a stick shift. It was easier to be around people like her sister Laura who was too phobic to even drive. Laura made Nina feel like a pioneer woman. How could one person feel alternately like a marshmallow and a pioneer woman with equal intensity, the only variable factor being who else was in the room? It was just a talent Nina had. During the past few years, however, the marshmallow feeling had become rarer, as most women tended to talk less about their daring exploits to attain true equality and more about how oppressive their lives were because their husbands didn't make enough money.

Now she had to get the discussion around to contact lenses. That would require conversational acrobatics, since it seemed as though John and Karen's argument was just warming up. They were like two male animals, getting ready to rear up on their haunches and lock horns.

"Karen," Nina said cheerfully, "are your eyes really that blue or are you wearing tinted contact lenses?" She felt like one of those Republican wives, gently steering the conversation to neutral territory whenever it got too heated.

"These are my eyes. But I never thought of them as particularly blue," she said with a hint of contempt. It occurred to Nina that Karen might have thought she was flirting with her. Karen looked like the kind of woman that other women get crushes on.

"What about you, John?" Nina continued. "Ever wear contact lenses?"

"No," he said.

"Me either," Nina said. She sat back against a rock to relax. Her investigation completed, she could look forward to a mostly downhill climb for the rest of the afternoon. This was sort of fun, actually. You got to ask people irrelevant personal questions without feeling pointless.

# Chapter
# Twelve

It was a washout," Nina told Williams. "I hate to sound like a woman in one of those magazine articles, but there were no men." She went into a mock whine on the last four words.

"None at all?"

"Well, that's not technically true. There were two men, but neither of them really counted." Nina and Williams were back in Susan's apartment. It had become sort of their private office. Nina wondered who was paying the rent and how long that person would continue to do so. It was something you thought about in New York, where monthly housing costs averaged half of everyone's take-home pay.

"Tell me about them," he said.

Nina described Mark Kurtz and John and her hike that day. Williams scribbled notes on a pad. "Don't you think we should rule them out?" she asked.

"I don't think you need to follow up on either of

them right now. But nothing in life gets ruled out. It all goes into the file.''

"So true.'' That's exactly what she felt like—a bulging file folder filled with half-written briefs and illegible internal memos. What she needed was someone to do some heavy-handed file maintenance. If only she could hit the delete button and dispatch all of her emotional baggage into whatever part of the universe was reserved for deleted material. She opened her mouth to share the thought, but stopped herself. She should watch it. Williams was not her therapist. He was not being paid eighty dollars an hour to listen to her explore her inner soul. Or to kvetch. (You couldn't do one without the other). She turned her attention away from her psyche back to the investigation. "So Saturday seems like it was a total waste, doesn't it?"

"Not really,'' he said. "You're going to have to pass yourself off as a hiker. So you might as well have some recent hiking experience to talk about.''

"I guess so. That is, if I have anyone to talk about it with. You know that I haven't gotten a single reply from the ad yet. Not that I'm taking it personally. You're half responsible for writing it. If no one wants to go out with me, it means they don't want to go out with you either.''

"I can live with that. But I'm not worried. It's still too early. You'll get some replies. The letters have to go to the magazine first and then be forwarded to you.''

"Maybe we should have rented a post office box. It would have been faster.''

"I didn't want to do that,'' Williams said, "because it wasn't the way Susan did it. I'm trying to replicate conditions here.''

"Do you think it would have made a difference?''

"It might. A box number might turn some people off. It might make it seem like the ad was placed by someone who ran personal ads all the time."

"Or a weirdo with a mail order business. That's what I think of when I see a post office box number. That some guy makes his living selling slice-and-dice machines on late-night television and places personal ads on the side."

"Actually, someone like that would be a good catch. Those direct marketing guys make a fortune."

"I'm still at the age, thank you very much, where I'm looking for a kindred soul, not a slice-and-dice king."

"You are? I thought you had already turned thirty-five."

"That's not funny. You see," Nina said, trying to be as condescending as possible, "self-deprecatory humor is a highly evolved art form. Deprecatory humor, on the other hand, is a vulgar form of expression generally indulged in by failing, aging comedians that can no longer get a decent booking in the Catskills during Passover."

"Not where I grew up. But we didn't call it deprecatory humor. We called it ranking people out."

"Well, of course. Ranking people out was a major art form in the Bronx. However, it is something you're supposed to outgrow." She thought back to childhood. You were never really supposed to say anything nice to anybody. Mothers swatted their kids, the boys hung out in the schoolyard and cursed, while the girls wrote nasty notes and ridiculed each other. And from this she was supposed to grow up into a wife who knew how to massage a husband's ego. And become a mother who instilled feelings of self-esteem at an early age. No wonder she steered clear of both roles. But the Bronx had been a good training ground for the law. Lots of practice in poking holes in other people's arguments.

"But you're right about turning thirty-five, you know," Nina continued. "I've been noticing a shift in my priorities lately. It seems like you spend the first thirty-five years worrying that you're not thin enough and the second thirty-five worrying that you're not rich enough."

"And the third thirty-five, should you be so lucky?"

"That you're not regular enough, I guess. Although I have a head start on that."

"Thank you for sharing that. You find out all sorts of interesting things in an investigation."

Here I go again, she said to herself. I can't get through five minutes of conversation without obsessing about my neuroses or, if denied the pleasure of discussing my mind, turning the conversation around to that other festering organ, my digestive tract. "You can put that in the file folder marked *Nina*. Meanwhile, what's this new stuff you told me on the phone that you just found?"

Williams reached into a stack on the desk and pulled out half a dozen back issues of *New York Magazine*. He opened one and flipped to the personals. "See? They're all marked up." He showed Nina that several of the ads had question marks next to them and that others had been checked off.

"This is great. Where did you find them?"

"Under her bed."

"Are they recent issues?"

"Pretty recent. The oldest one is from June."

"So we could answer these? I mean, the magazine would still forward a letter to these guys?"

"The deal is that as long as the letters come in, they'll be sent on."

Nina took a look at one of the ads that Susan had

checked off. She read it out loud to Williams. " 'Retread,' " she read. " 'Ready to try again. Divorced man, late thirties, Ivy, Wall Street. I love the outdoors and my kids. Looking for a like-minded woman of independent spirit. Looks somewhat important.' I'm surprised she answered this one."

"Why?"

"This guy is clearly paying heavy alimony. 'Of independent spirit.' You know what that means. He never wants to pick up another check."

"Susan was looking for someone to pick up the checks?"

"At least a goodly portion of them."

"Hmmmm." Williams was looking a little sour.

"Look," Nina explained, "in this town you see all these women wearing four-inch heels because the only movement demanded of them is scampering into their limousines. You get tired of putting your own token in the slot all the time."

"What about the fact that he was divorced? That didn't bother her?"

"There is a somewhat popular theory that men who haven't married by their late thirties never will. That you're better off with a retread, as he refers to himself here. In fact, I think it was last winter when Susan was on her furniture store kick."

"What do you mean?" he asked.

"She'd hang around furniture stores to meet men, on the theory that any man out by himself shopping for furniture was probably recently divorced and ripe for the picking. Hot off the press, if you will."

"I see. But apparently she didn't confine herself to retreads. Most of the ads she marked off didn't specify that the men had been divorced."

"It wasn't a requirement. Susan was pretty open-minded. Too open-minded most of the time."

"This last time, anyway."

"Right." Nina pressed her palms together and rested her chin on her hands. "Too open-minded."

"She must have been. Because I've read all these ads over and over, and no clear pattern emerges. Some say Jewish, some say hiking, some say divorced. But others don't. They're all over the place."

"Everything's there except discreet afternoons, huh?"

"What does that mean?" he asked.

"I see you're not a regular reader."

He grinned. "No, I'm not. Anyway, maybe you can see some pattern that I can't. Something more subtle. I brought copies for you to read. Study them for a while. See what you come up with. Then we'll draft some responses next week."

"Okay."

"Do you know if Susan used to type or handwrite her replies?"

"I don't really know. But believe me, even if she wrote them by hand, there's no point in my doing that."

"Why not?"

"Anyone who was attracted to Susan's handwriting certainly wouldn't go for mine. Susan could have gotten into art school on the basis of her handwriting alone. Mine looks more like the scrawl of an arthritic drunk." Nina actually was sort of proud of her messy penmanship. There was something agreeably macho about it. No one would ever mistake her for someone who went to Catholic school. Not that there was really much chance of that anyway.

"Okay, you can type them."

Nina never felt like she had gotten much out of law school. She had never fully absorbed the historical legal implications of the British property system, or grasped the wondrous uniqueness of a system of common, as opposed to codified, law. And a contract always seemed like a long, dull document as opposed to a living, breathing meeting of the minds. But one thing she did learn in law school—you don't do your own typing.

"How about this?" she said, summoning up a brisk supervisory manner. A manner that did not come naturally. "I'll draft a basic form response and then mark up the copies to send out. And you'll edit them and get them typed." She knew it couldn't be like the cop shows, with Williams at an old manual typewriter, doing his own hunting and pecking.

"Sounds good. Could you be ready by tomorrow evening?"

"Tomorrow is bad." The day after tomorrow was her deadline for submitting a memorandum in opposition to a motion to dismiss in one of her cases. She felt a small wave of panic swell and crash. Nina tried to be the kind of person who thrived on being overextended, on having too much to do and too little time in which to do it. But she secretly believed herself to be the kind of person who would thrive on more time, more money, and fewer demands. She would probably never know. "How about Wednesday instead?"

"That's fine." Of course he granted her the adjournment. What was he going to do, fire her?

"It'll be fun," she said. "We'll pretend that we're Susan while we're editing the ads. Like Method actors. We'll fill abalone shells with potpourri and put on big earrings and spray ourselves with Obsession perfume and sit around, eating rice cakes."

"You mean those styrofoam things? I'll pass."

"But you don't mind the earrings and the perfume?" She pictured Williams in drag. He was a big guy, and she couldn't help thinking of the dancing hippo in *Fantasia*.

"Whatever it takes," he said. And she got the feeling that he meant it.

# Chapter
# Thirteen

Nina took the ads to her office the next day. Whenever she needed to feel organized, she took things to work. Bills to be paid, thank you notes to be written, tasks that seemed hopelessly overwhelming at home seemed like light recreation in the office. They were, compared to the endless stream of client problems she had to untangle. There was something illicit about writing a check in the office. Stealing time gave her a thrill, like having sex in an elevator. Which was why she kept dental floss in her office desk. Office flossing was as close as she could get to the proverbial secretary under the desk.

There was more to it than that, actually. Offices made her feel functional. Even though she was far from having everything under control at work, she never found herself sinking into the kind of hopeless despair that she felt when she spent too much time at home. In the office you could always pop in next door and be distracted by the life of a colleague. People paid therapists and hookers and the phone company for human contact. Nina considered herself lucky. She had a corridor full of like-minded people who were always willing to talk—which was probably why she had never changed jobs. She was afraid that if she went somewhere else she wouldn't be popular anymore. That she'd be back in junior high school, for all intents and purposes, sitting alone at a cafeteria table.

And at home it was just you and your dirty laundry and soiled thoughts. Nina had never learned the trick of staying at home, had never conquered her fear of the house, her *casaphobia*. Other women seemed to thrive at home. Neither her mother nor her sister appeared to have any problem making their kitchen their base of operations. But Nina was someone who needed a humming Xerox machine and two phone lines to make her feel comfortable. A dishwasher and a microwave just didn't do it. Not to mention the fact that office eating required ordering out, a more complicated process than just opening the refrigerator. Although there were days, especially when she was working on a brief, when the delivery men seemed to pass each other in the hall.

Today could have been one of those days. The entire morning evaporated before she even had a chance to start drafting her memo in opposition to the motion to dismiss. Actually, drafting was probably too grand a word for what she was doing. She always thought that the real course they should require in the first year of law school, instead of Legal Writing, was Cutting and Pasting. Then you could graduate up to Legal Boilerplate and on to Advanced Forms.

Nina cut and pasted for a while. But she didn't want the whole thing to be boilerplate. She always tried to include at least one lofty sentiment in her papers, and also tried to tailor it to each case. She figured she owed the client at least that. But nothing was coming here. It was a good case: A grandmother had been denied welfare benefits at her hearing, even though she was the sole support and caretaker of her four grandchildren. The hearing officer had been preoccupied with an emergency phone call he had received during the proceedings. Nina had a feeling she was going to have to appeal this one and she had been right. The written denial of benefits had misconstrued the facts and misapplied the law.

Nina sat back and tried to let her lofty sentiments flow, but she seemed to have run dry. It seemed like a natural case for some truly creative writing. The children's mother had died, the identities of their fathers were unclear, the grandmother was all they had. She lived on Supplemental Security Income, due to a heart condition that prevented her from working. SSI was Social Security disability for people who didn't have enough covered quarters to qualify for Social Security. As the guardian of these four children, the grandmother was entitled to an Aid to Dependent Children grant to supplement her SSI. The ADC grant had been denied. The hearing officer had not been convinced that she was actually taking care of these children, which was ridiculous. If he had been paying attention during the hearing instead of talking on the phone, he would have seen that the evidence of the relationship was uncontroverted.

She felt a lofty sentiment coming on. The Ghetto Grandmother—the linchpin of the nuclear family. A parade of dignified elderly women marched through her mind. They marched home from their jobs—as home attendants or nurses' aides or some other glorified variation of domestic—and picked up the grandba-

bies from day care and changed endless diapers and
warmed endless bottles on into the night. Then got
dressed the next morning and started all over again.

Nina thought about her sister Laura, the doctor's
wife, with her career as a part-time furniture restorer
with a full-time nanny. Laura was convinced that having conceived a third child was the most radical act
imaginable. Then Nina thought about herself, ambivalent about motherhood, ambivalent about marriage,
even about going out on a goddamn date. So much
for marching forward with dignity.

Thinking about dating dried up whatever stream of
lofty sentiments might have started flowing. She put
away her memo and pulled out Susan's personal ads.
The first one had a question mark next to it. It started
off with "Handsome Christian Businessman." Was
Susan kidding? She went on to the next. That one
started off with "Caring, Unpretentious Investment
Banker." It also had a question mark next to it.
Maybe Susan's question marks didn't mean "Should
I answer this?" Maybe they meant "Is this guy for
real?" Nina skipped down to a check mark. "I Like
Jazz," this one read. "Hiking upstate, antiquing in
the Village, and subscribing to the ballet. I'm looking
for a very smart, very witty, very kind, very real
woman to share my life with. Age and religion unim-
portant. Should have some red in her hair. Bio/photo.
NYM T2847." Nina wondered what kind of guy
would consider age and religion less important than
hair color. Susan sometimes had some red in her hair
and sometimes not. It depended on how recently she
had hit the henna.

By the time Nina finished reading the ads, having
some red in one's hair seemed like a minimal request.
The popular formula seemed to be to string together
three or four glowing adjectives, telling as little about

yourself as possible, and then go right into a long list of the requirements that you sought in a mate. The ads were often punctuated at the end with what you wanted out of the situation. Which might be to share your life, to make a commitment, to marry and have a family, to stare deeply into each other's soul or—in the case of the caring, unpretentious investment banker—to cruise the Caribbean this winter on his thirty-nine-foot sailboat.

The adjectives the men used to describe themselves were meaningless and interchangeable: dynamic, successful, rugged, sensitive, handsome, athletic—none conveyed a really clear image. But their requirements were sharply specific. It reminded her of a lawyer she had gone out with once. The date had taken place in an Italian restaurant. His choice, of course. He had cross-examined the waiter mercilessly. Were the tomatoes in the mozzarella appetizer fresh or sundried? Did the seafood salad contain squid? If not, he wasn't interested. What kind of vinegar did they use in the house dressing? Balsamic was fine, plain red wine vinegar was no good. Lemon juice was an acceptable substitute, but only if fresh. Bottled was no good. What about the lettuce? Radicchio and arugula were okay, but he could not abide endive. Were there wild mushrooms adorning the veal chop, or the flavorless, pedestrian kind that one bought in twelve-ounce cartons? By the time he turned his attention away from the menu and toward Nina, she was ready to bolt. Naturally, she was similarly dissected. How long in therapy? A psychiatrist or a psychologist? Certainly not an MSW, he trusted. Ever been in group? Men and women in the group, he hoped. Mostly women? What was the ratio? Four-to-three was acceptable, two-to-one was not.

Nina wondered what the trick to answering these

ads was. Maybe it was to fight fire with fire. To use those same elusive adjectives about yourself and list your own ridiculous requirements. She suspected that the real trick to answering was to send a photo of yourself in a black leather skirt no longer than a standard-size legal pad. Well, that might have done for Susan, but not for Nina. Any photo she sent would have to be a head shot.

Anyhow, she was going to have to describe herself so that she could also be Susan. She would be okay on the age, religion, neighborhood, and background. The career and physical description she would have to fudge. She picked up her legal pad and started drafting. It wasn't that different from motion papers, actually. She wrote a few boilerplate paragraphs and then basically started to cut and paste. Before she knew it, she had mass-produced a stack of responses.

She liked her basic format. She thought it quite clever. Each response started with: "Hi. This is my first time answering a *New York Magazine* ad because yours is the first I've ever read that doesn't include any of the following words: *triathlon, quality, sophisticated, GQ, entrepreneur, yacht, CEO or St. Tropez.* (She double-checked each ad to make sure that this was really the case. *Sophisticated,* however, appeared with such regularity that she had to drop it from her master). Also there is no clever play on words involving deal making or real estate. Best of all, you didn't start all of the words in your ad with the same letter."

She went on to describe herself as being in a helping profession. She figured it was basically true, not that she often felt that she was actually helping anybody. But it was much closer to Susan's job description than using the *L* word. The physical description she limited to *attractive,* unless it seemed necessary to add something more specific. The guy who loved jazz, for example, was assured that she had a modicum of red in her hair. She really did, assuming you were looking at her outside in direct sunlight. She went heavy on the indoor/outdoor stuff and stressed her desire for a real relationship. But only with someone who wears contact lenses, she thought.

She polished and polished during the afternoon. It was a great way to avoid working on her motion papers. She ended up having to stay up until three in the morning to finish her memo. But the following evening, when she showed her stack of replies to Williams, she was quite proud of them.

He read a few of them through. "We're going to have to cut the first paragraph," he finally said.

"No," Nina wailed. "It's my best work. It's innovative, it's daring, it's fresh."

"You think anybody is going to believe that you've never answered a *New York Magazine* ad before?"

"But it's true."

"It's like trying to pass yourself off as a virgin. After a certain age, even if it's true, it loses its appeal."

Nina felt her negotiating juices starting to run. "How about this? We'll change 'this is my first time answering a *New York Magazine* ad because yours is the first I've ever read that doesn't include any of the following words' to 'this is the first time in ages that I've answered a *New York Magazine* ad because it's so rare to find one that doesn't include any of the following words.' How would that be? More believable?"

"I guess so," Williams said.

"Am I giving out my home phone number on these?"

"I've thought about that. I think it's unfair for you

to have to go through that, so I've arranged for a separate line to be installed in your house. We'll have it taken out when this is all over."

"That's very considerate, but sort of pointless. If I'm giving out my real name, all you have to do is look me up in the phone book."

"You don't have to do that, you know."

"Do what?"

"Use your real name. You can use another name. Or at least a different last name."

Nina thought about it. "I don't think I could do that. It would be like getting married and changing my name. I couldn't imagine it."

"It wouldn't be like getting married and changing your name at all. We're talking about going on a few dates, that's all. And you could still be Nina. You'd just be Nina Hershkowitz instead of Nina Fischman."

"I couldn't be Nina Hershkowitz. Not even for one date."

"How about this? We'll give you the new phone line and you'll just be Nina. You'll tell them you had a strange experience once and you feel funny about revealing your last name."

"Nina X, woman of mystery. I don't know if I can pull it off. I'm not the most secretive person in the world. Ask any of my old friends that are no longer talking to me."

"Well, you're going to have to put a little effort into trying not to get into trouble. This is a hunt for a real killer, not a fun singles murder mystery weekend."

"Okay, I'll try to be a little elusive." Being elusive did not come naturally. She found the quality . . . well, elusive. It would probably be good practice for dating, anyhow. And might help in court. If nothing else, it wouldn't hurt her poker game.

# Chapter
# Fourteen

Nina generally wasn't much of a consumer complainer. She never seemed to notice that anything was wrong with an item, while other people sputtered and fumed and returned. It was probably why she never had really taken to litigation. The born litigators had an internal flame of righteous indignation that burned eternally.

But even a wimp like herself could tell, she thought as she sorted through the stack of replies her ad had finally generated, that she was holding the biggest pile of consumer fraud she had seen since her law school civil advocacy clinic. Back then she had been afforded the opportunity to help out on the discovery in a class action suit against Rio Alegre, a land sales outfit which sold lots in the New Mexican desert. The president of Rio Alegre had considered truth in advertising and full and fair disclosure to be somewhat alien concepts. The guys who had answered her ad certainly ran a close second.

Not all of them, actually. There were a fair number of somewhat sweet replies from guys with their own air conditioning installation businesses in New Jersey or from baggage handlers at Kennedy Airport. Their letters seemed free of exaggeration, if not of spelling errors. But those guys were not what Susan had been looking for when she moved to New York. And Nina would have been very surprised if that's who Susan had been with on her last hike.

So Nina eliminated most of the blue-collar responses and concentrated on the professionals and their public relations bulletins. The lawyers were easy to check on. All you had to do was look them up in Martindale Hubbell. Most attorneys, at least the ones in the private sector, had a bio listed there. Nina had found a used copy at a book sale once and had dragged it home for yenta purposes. Now it was coming in handy. She chose a promising-looking letter and opened the big, tattered book. You could pretty much figure out how old these guys really were, since the bio included the year they had graduated from law school.

This fellow had apparently clipped his age by at least ten years, unless he had graduated from Brooklyn Law School the same year that he was bar mitzvahed. And he hadn't even used his real first name. He had altered it from Depression-era Morton to a more postwar Martin. Morton/Martin apparently felt that this subtle vowel play lent him a dash of glamor that had probably eluded him since he sprouted his first facial blemish during Truman's administration. Nina decided to pass on old Mort. At his age there was a natural shift away from contact lenses towards bifocals.

What was it that Susan had said about the hiker? Good haircut, good build, good wardrobe, and contact lenses. She tried making a checklist as she went through the replies, but she didn't get anywhere with it. Very few had sent pictures, and all those that had, had good builds. Otherwise they wouldn't have sent photos. And most of them were wearing jeans in the shots, standing in the woods or, in a few cases, in front of an expensive car. And none of them were wearing glasses. Maybe she should call them all up and cross-examine them on these issues. It would be too nervy of her, she thought, to question them on their physical appearance before they were even granted an audience. Although she had a feeling that men in these situations did it all the time.

She'd have to go on instinct. She had known Susan as well as she had known anyone. Nina should be able to figure out which of these guys would have appealed to her. But it was tricky, since Susan had been trying to force herself into a new, more result-oriented dating pattern. So it was more like figuring out which of these guys Susan would have thought should have appealed to her. You had to operate on several levels at once. The most likely candidate was someone to whom Susan felt she should be attracted and, as a bonus, actually found appealing. Nina divided the responses into a "should" and "should not" pile and then subdivided the "should" pile into "would" and "would not" piles. The "should/would" pile was the smallest. But there were a fair number of replies there.

She called Williams. "I've sorted out the most likely responses," she told him.

"Based on what?" he asked.

She considered explaining about the "should/would" pile, but thought the conversation might turn into an Abbott and Costello "Who's on First?" routine. "Based on my judgment," she simply said.

"Well, in that case, I'd better have a look, hadn't I?"

"I thought I explained to you about deprecatory humor."

"Right. Let's go over them anyway. How many finalists did you come up with?"

"About a dozen."

"What do they do for a living?"

"A couple of lawyers, bankers, advertising, like that. And I think there's a few computer guys in there. I can't say exactly. I haven't kept a running tab on them."

"And where do they live?"

"Mostly 212 area codes. But at least one 718, 914, and 201." That probably meant Brooklyn, Westchester, and New Jersey.

"Do they fit her description?"

"I can't tell. Only one of them sent a photo, and he looks all right to me. Actually, it's only a Xerox of a photo. And you can't tell if someone is wearing contact lenses from a Xerox of a photo."

"Do they mention hiking?"

"A few mention it specifically. All of them give at least an honorable mention to the outdoors. Do you want me to start with the ones that like to hike?"

"I'd at least like to take a look at the letters before you do anything."

"Okay," Nina said. "But you'll be disappointed. There's no psychotic handwriting, no drool stains, no bloody fingerprints. Just a bunch of self-obsessed yuppies touting their virtues. Which, on some level, I suppose, can be more horrifying than bloody fingerprints."

"It's an all-yuppie crowd?"

"I'd say so."

"Why is that?" he asked. "Is that all we got? Or

does that reflect your taste? Or is it what Susan was attracted to?"

"It's what Susan was looking for."

"I guess it's naive of me to think there should be any parallel between what she was attracted to and what she was looking for."

How should she explain this to him? They had never set out to seek the conventional. She and Susan had spent years cultivating their imaginations and independence. But then the rules had changed on them, and there didn't seem to be anything else to do but follow them. And she had found herself a lawyer dating lawyers. Susan had avoided conventionality for years by living in strange places and becoming involved with strange men. However, in the end she had come home, enrolled in graduate school, and started seeking suits.

Lately Nina felt that it seemed harder than ever to live an exciting and independent life, at least without a trust fund. It seemed to have gone out of fashion, except for her mother, and Ida had to spend seven decades paying dues before she got to live the life she wanted. Nina wondered how much of this was a woman's issue. Maybe it was easier for a man in this day and age to pull off being Simone de Beauvoir.

"I'm sorry," Nina said to Williams. "It's a sign of the times. Maybe this new decade will be better than the last."

"So far I'm not encouraged."

Nina thought about what it would be like to be black and male in this country. Existential angst was still a bourgeois privilege. Although worrying about not being Simone de Beauvoir was better than worrying about breaking a nail, she supposed. But when you thought about how people really lived, maybe there wasn't that much difference. "I'll drop these off tomorrow," she said, because she didn't know what else to say.

"That's okay. I'll have someone pick them up." Nina felt a small pang of disappointment. Once she analyzed it, she realized that she had been looking forward to seeing him.

# Chapter
# Fifteen

Here she was. Williams had given her the go-ahead on her "should/would" pile. But not before he had chuckled as he read the letters and murmured something about white boy con artists.

Meanwhile, Nina had chatted pleasantly on the telephone with eleven men. Two had bowed out. One was going on an extended trip to New Zealand, and the other had become engaged during the past week. Or maybe her voice turned them off, she couldn't tell. Anyway, they weren't available for inspection. Another four claimed never to have hiked. This could also have been untrue, but she bumped them down to round two anyway. Which left five finalists, all of whom would be glad to meet her for a drink—and a hike, if things worked out.

So here she was, in a bar of a restaurant that she'd never been in before. And probably never would be in again. It was a high-ticket joint, filled with the kind of people that she always thought existed only in magazines, until she came face to face with them, as she occasionally did. Nina considered herself a New York woman—she wore black and had her hair cut on Madison Avenue. And to a trucker's wife from Des Moines, she could probably pass for one. But a more sophisticated eye could spot the differences. She wasn't really a New York Woman, the kind with a capital *W*, like the magazine. For example, Nina was still carrying a Coach bag, which, in public sector lady lawyer circles, was *de rigueur*. The crowd at the bar, however, had moved on to Fendi years ago. And they might have their hair cut by the same guy that Nina used, but when he said every six weeks to them, they took him seriously. Instead of mentally doubling it, like she did. And a lot of these women wore high heels. There seemed to be some reverse bell curve for high-heel wearing. The women who made under twenty-five thousand a year all wore them. The ones who made between twenty-five and seventy wore flats, but the real upscale ones wore heels as high as the secretaries'. Nina used to cling to the myth that the height of a woman's heels, as well as the length of her nails, was inversely proportional to her intelligence. But in a place like this, her flats made her feel like a cuddly little dachshund among sleekly groomed Afghan hounds.

The restaurant looked like it got a haircut every six weeks as well. This was way beyond fern bar. In fact, there wasn't a plant to be seen anywhere. Earthtones had been banished in favor of cooler colors, postmodern grays, purples, and blacks. The tables and chairs were cutting-edge Milanese. Gray leather was the fabric of preference, paired with a lot of brushed aluminum. When had it first been discovered, she wondered, that you could brush aluminum. On each table sat one dark purple tulip in its own vase. It wasn't actually a vase, it was more of a contraption. The base of the contraption was a slab of white marble, with a depression sunk into it that served as a water reservoir. Rising from one side of the base was a black wire that shot up about twelve inches, swooped out over the reservoir, turned back in and paralleled itself back down to the base. The trick was to thread the tulip stem through the wire and drop the cut end into the water. The wire propped the flower up. It had the exact right combination of minimal utilitarianism and elegance that today's design cognoscenti demanded.

Which Nina was not one of. She had to acknowledge that the vase was extremely clever. It was a good way to make a design statement without buying more than one flower. But it was so coldly clinical. It looked like an appliance that a gynecologist or an ophthalmological surgeon would use. It seemed to represent a generational syndrome, which was to rid your life of all the schmaltz, get lean and mean, and then add a child or two to put the warmth back in. It seemed misguided, like refining wheat flour until it was stripped of its nutrients, and then fortifying it with synthetic vitamins and minerals. Yet this Wonder Bread approach prevailed.

Another way to look at it was as the latest stage in an age of specialization. You kept your home looking like a leather bar and your clothing looking like a science-fiction movie wardrobe. Then loaded up the nursery with hundreds of stuffed animals and old-fashioned wooden jigsaw puzzles and chintz crib bumpers. And decked the kids out in Victorian finery. And spoke in a calculated monotone all day and like a three-year-old when you got home at night. And manipulated clients and staff and opposing counsel from Monday to Friday and then fled to the country on the weekends to spend it with your family, instilling decent values. It seemed hypocritical to Nina, but also horrifyingly appealing. Emotionally efficient. Which, after all, was the idea of specialization.

The crowd in the restaurant seemed a bit young for chintz crib bumpers. They were probably still in the seven-day-a-week mean and lean stage. It was a Friday night, so the crib bumpers had probably all fled to the country. The crowd looked good, though; she had to give them that. The men as well as the women. Both sexes dressed alike. The men wore flats, of course. No reverse bell curve for them, except maybe for hair oil. She had never figured out why investment bankers seemed to grease their hair back like bikers did. But both the men and the women wore the same elegantly tailored, loose-fitting slacks. And tieless shirts buttoned up to the neck in textured silk or rayon. The women had fabulous three-hundred-dollar silver pins at the necks of their shirts. Instead of the fabulous pins, the men wore three-hundred-dollar silver belt buckles. There was a lot of reptile skin wrapped around the feet and waists of both sexes. There was probably more reptile skin in this place than in the entire reptile house in the Bronx Zoo.

As she scrutinized the room, she looked for him. Door number one. He was late enough to be cool. He said she would recognize him by his round eyeglasses. He was an architect. Ever since Corbusier, he had explained, a lot of architects wore round glasses. They were really the only ones who could get away with it. If you meet a man wearing round glasses and he's not an architect, then he's a putz, he had told her over the phone. He hadn't used that word, but that was the idea. She pictured a large office filled with men and women all wearing round glasses—an architectural Farkel family. She had asked him if the contrapositive was true—that if you were an architect, but didn't wear round glasses, did that make you a putz also. No, he had said. That was okay.

Nina didn't know any architects. It was a profession that had quickly shot up from a grindy, underpaid one to being glamorous. Today's rock stars, the magazines proclaimed. She really should have ruled this guy out. Susan had said contact lenses, not round eyeglasses. But maybe he usually wore lenses and the round frames were an occasional affectation, an easy way to describe himself to a blind date. And she had already made the arrangements before he had mentioned the glasses. Besides, this would be her first date with an architect. What with them being such hot properties and all, she didn't have the heart to cancel.

There he was, a little bald, but otherwise looking very much like everyone else in the place. Brown slacks, black shirt and a silver belt buckle in the shape of a crescent moon. He recognized her immediately. She had told him she'd be wearing a leopard-print headband. Nina felt a little stupid wearing such a fashion item, but it was an easy and emotionally neutral way to describe yourself without having to go into sensitive topics such as weight or how much gray you had in your hair.

"Nina," he said without inflection, and shook her hand. "Shall we sit at a table?" There were a few tables scattered around the bar. They were deliberately undersized and lacked the purple tulips of the regular tables, so as to give a visual cue that it was all right to sit there with your drink and not order dinner. The same message that a bowl of goldfish crackers and a stack of cocktail napkins would give in a less-classy joint.

As he led her over to the table, she ran him through her mental checklist. He was certainly well dressed. Not only was the belt buckle made of precious metal, but the end of the belt that got pushed through the loops was covered with a silver triangle that matched the buckle. It was a small detail, but according to Mies van der Rohe, God was in the details. He had a good enough build. Not one of these tall, broad shouldered types, but small and wiry and muscular. A natural runt that had transformed himself into acceptability with the help of a personal, or impersonal, trainer.

A cocktail waitress immediately came over to their table. It was a little hard to tell she was a waitress, since she wore the same shoes, pants, and alligator belt as all the customers. She could have been a friendly soul that came over to chat. Then Nina realized that her shirt, instead of being textured raw silk in an interesting jewel tone, was white cotton. That was what was supposed to clue you in. "Would you like another?" the waitress asked Nina, who was down to an inch of beer.

"Okay. I'm drinking Heineken," she said.

The architect, whose name was Victor, settled in for a serious talk with the waitress. "What do you have that's unblended?" he asked.

"Glenfiddich," she answered.

"Besides Glenfiddich," he said with just the tiniest bit of impatience. As if Glenfiddich were the obvious and she should have been able to tell that he was a man who did not seek out the obvious.

"I'll have to check." The waitress went over to talk to the bartender. Victor gave Nina a small, long-suffering smile. He sat back to wait for the woman to return with the information he had requested. He didn't want to start another conversation until this important matter had been resolved.

Luckily she returned forthwith, for Nina couldn't stand silences, deliberate or otherwise. "We've got Glenlivet," the waitress said hopefully.

Victor gave a tiny snort that made it clear that Glenlivet was just as painfully obvious as Glenfiddich. "What about Macallan?" he asked.

"Sorry." The waitress tilted her head in sympathy. She must be used to this sort of display, Nina thought.

"Laphroag? Glen Grant?"

"No, just Glenfiddich and Glenlivet."

Nina waited it out calmly. She had never been out with a single malt freak before, but she had sat through enough similar conversations in Japanese restaurants while some sushi fetishist cross-examined the waitress endlessly about *futomaki* and reverse *futomaki* to know that all you could do was wait for it to be over.

"I'll have a Courvoisier," he proclaimed, a martyr of the highest order. He sat in disappointed silence for a few seconds, then turned his attention to Nina. "You know," he said, "you look exactly like the sister of someone I went to school with. You wouldn't happen to have a brother who went to Andover, would you?"

"Afraid not. No brother at all. Besides, we're strictly a Bronx Science family." Nina smiled. Victor did not.

"Is that where you're from? The Bronx?"

"Yup. Born and bred."

He looked at her as if she were a tumbler of Glenfiddich. "I've never before met anyone who actually grew up there."

Well, cross this guy off the list. Of course, he might

be lying to throw her off. She supposed he could have spent weekends listening to Susan regale him with amusing anecdotes about her Bronx childhood before bumping her off. But judging by the way he was looking at her, Nina tended to doubt it.

The waitress returned with their drinks. Nina finished off her inch of Heineken and reached urgently for the next. She had a feeling that she was going to need a six-pack to get through an evening with this guy. Better turn the conversation away from lineage to career, she thought. The great equalizer. That was the good thing about New York. Unlike most other cities, if you clawed your way up, it didn't matter so much where you went to school or where your parents went to school or whether your grandparents were born here or over there. Although Nina had a feeling that a mere law degree would not constitute sufficient clawing, as far as Victor was concerned. Especially since she continued to languish in the public sector.

"Do you work for a firm?" she asked.

"No, I have my own business. I work out of my home."

"Do you have any employees?"

"No, it's just me and my office machines."

"Doesn't that get lonely? And boring?"

"Not really. I break up the day by lifting weights in the morning and doing an hour on the Stairmaster in the afternoon."

"But don't you miss seeing people?"

"Well, I manage to date on a regular basis."

Nina tried to imagine what it would be like to rely solely upon dating for human interaction and emotional sustenance. She had never considered dating a particularly nurturing experience. This guy was starving himself to death. He was an emotional anorexic.

And an hour on the Stairmaster seemed excessive. A yuppie form of bulimia. Maybe this was how men evidenced forms of eating disorders.

She tried another topic. "Do you get to hike much?" she asked.

"Hardly ever," he said.

"Me either," she said.

"Although," he continued, "last summer I did manage to do a week-long backpack in the Canadian Rockies. It was really beautiful. You haven't really hiked until you've put on a pair of crampons and crossed a mile-wide glacier all by yourself. Now, that's what I call hiking."

"It sounds strenuous for someone who doesn't get to go hiking regularly. I've found that the only way to stay in shape for hiking is to hike. How did you manage?"

"I walked up fifteen flights of stairs every day for a month with five-pound ankle weights on each leg."

This guy was definitely bent, thought Nina. Guys like that made her want to go home and sit in front of the television and eat frozen Milky Way bars and never go to the gym again. But mostly they made her want to go home, which she did as soon as she gracefully could.

# Chapter
# Sixteen

Door Number Two seemed more promising. For one thing, he had suggested that they meet at La Fortuna, which was familiar turf to Nina. For a long time it had been the only place to get a cup of cappuccino in the West Seventies, when the neighborhood was still mostly filled with Greek coffee shops. Now it was the only place you could get a cup of cappuccino without a ten-dollar minimum. Unless you felt like being tortured at Eclair, over on Seventy-second Street. The problem with Eclair was that it was filled with old Jewish ladies. Not the Ida Fischman kind, who viewed the neighborhood as a wonderful step up from the Bronx, but the ill-tempered kind, who viewed the last fifty years as a terrible step down from Vienna.

La Fortuna was festive, with small marble tables, and opera playing in the background. Over the years, Nina had logged in a lot of hours there. It was a great place for eavesdropping. Nina could sit by herself, toying with her espresso and her *New Yorker,* and hear the greatest conversations. Not only because the tables were close together, but because the people spoke her language. The crowd packed in at the marble tables were saying things worth hearing.

Nina was a discriminating eavesdropper. As soon as the conversation veered off towards junk bonds and tennis camp, her attention wandered. But the La Fortuna regulars never failed her. They talked endlessly about relationships, diets, their mothers, the same topics over and over for years. Topics that Nina never tired of, whether or not she was actually in the conversation. This was the Old Upper West Side. People who would be in therapy forever. People who never moved on. Her people.

So far, this guy—whose name was Patrick—seemed to be pretty easy to relate to. They were on their second round of *biscotti,* and he hadn't cross-examined the waitress at all. Besides, he was cute. Very cute. Irish with that unbeatable combination of black hair and blue eyes and pink cheeks that makes everything look blacker and bluer and pinker. And instead of a textured silk shirt buttoned up to the collar, he wore his plaid wool shirt open at the neck and rolled up at the sleeves, exposing just the right amount of arm and chest hair.

Patrick was explaining to Nina how he had left the District Attorney's office to set up a criminal practice with his law school roommate and now found himself doing less law and more investigative work. "What happened was that I fell in love with my car phone," he said.

"Tell me about it." He seemed to have a good narrative line.

"It was love at first sight. It got so that I couldn't bear to sit at a desk any more. I wanted to conduct all my business from my car. If I didn't have a moving vista in front of me I felt confined. Staring at my wall calendar was death.''

"How did your partner feel about that?"

"He was getting pretty pissed at my inability to sit still. To keep him off my back, I stopped farming out the investigations and started doing them myself.''

"Like what?" Nina pictured him in a trenchcoat, popping flashbulbs at a cheating husband.

"Since we had mostly criminal clients, there was a lot of witness interviewing. Which was perfect for me. I'd get to hang around bars and donut shops in jeans. It was like reliving my adolescence. Then I started getting referrals from other lawyers for more sophisticated stuff, like locating missing persons for estates. I find that stuff interesting. I spent quite a bit of time recently finding the birth mother of a client who had been adopted thirty years ago. It was an extremely difficult case. But exciting.''

"And that's the sort of thing you do now?"

"Yeah. My partner and I broke up last year and since then I don't even bill myself as a lawyer anymore. In fact, I advertise in the *Law Journal* as a legal investigator.''

She'd seen it, now that he had mentioned it. Not that she was an avid *Law Journal* reader, but you had to check it every now and then to see which judge had done what to your motion. He ran a nice little display ad—Patrick Brennan, J.D. Legal Investigations. He had a downtown office, if she remembered correctly. Three- or four-something Broadway.

Nina sat back to assess. He was definitely cool. So cool, in fact, that she could barely stand it. She noticed herself playing with her hair. In her experience, hair playing was generally a ploy to alleviate

sexual tension. "So are you a regular in this joint?"
she asked.

"I used to be. When I lived in the neighborhood."

"How long ago was that?"

"It's been about three years, I guess. I got married
five years ago and we lived in my apartment for two.
Then we bought a house up in Rockland."

"Oh."

"The marriage broke up right after that," he added
quickly.

"Before or after you fell in love with your car
phone?"

"Everything seemed to happen at once. I'll admit
that the divorce might have had something to do with
my need to drive around endlessly. She ran off with
the family vet, so I ran off with the family car
phone."

"The family veterinarian? That's a new one."

"It was new to me. It made sense, actually. You
see, we were having problems and there was a lot of
yelling going on. Apparently it was making the cat
nervous because she licked herself practically bald.
We didn't know what was going on. At the time we
thought it might be a nutritional deficiency or something. So my wife took the cat to the vet to see what
was wrong with her. He diagnosed it as excessive
grooming due to stress or boredom. He wanted to
put the cat on valium."

"Did this really happen? It sounds like the beginning of a bad Jap joke."

"Apparently this was his diagnosis. I don't know,
because I wasn't there. Anyway, my wife didn't want
a tranked-out cat, so she said she refused to medicate
it. The vet started probing a bit to see what could be
leading to this excessive grooming problem. So my

wife starts pouring her heart out and the next thing you know, she's moved into his condo."

"You're still in the house?"

"Yup. I got the marital abode. She got the cat."

"Did you think about moving back to the neighborhood?"

"Sure. I had the house on the market for a while. But you know, this neighborhood had changed too much for me. I didn't really think it was my kind of place anymore."

This was the fourth most popular topic of conversation in La Fortuna. Right after relationships, diets, and mothers. The Neighborhood Was Not The Same. Someone should teach it as a course at the Learning Annex: How the neighborhood had changed, why the neighborhood had changed, and what to expect in the future. You could start with a lecture on seminal events. It had a lot of dramatic potential. "On a hot summer day back in 1977, Julee Rosso and Sheila Lukins sat down with their lawyer, who held in his hands a file that contained a lease agreement for a small Columbus Avenue storefront. Written across the front of the file were the words *The Silver Palate*. Three small words that would mean more than anyone could ever imagine." Or you could get guest lecturers to give history lessons. Like the Miss Grimble lady talking about how she had to keep Doberman Pinschers in the store when she first opened because the West Seventies were so dangerous. Or interview Michael Weinstein about his decision to open the Museum Cafe back when Gray's Papaya was the only place to eat.

There was almost something obligatory about this topic of conversation. If you got through a first date without once discussing how much the Upper West Side had changed, your souls hadn't really mingled.

So when Patrick brought up the topic, Nina felt the warm glow that always preceded the mingling of souls. "Oh, has the neighborhood changed? I hadn't noticed." She gave him a mock smile.

He gave her an immediate laugh that let her know that he knew she hadn't been serious, not for a minute. That they understood each other. "You've decided to stick it out?" he said. That was good. He was asking her a question about herself and it had been less than an hour. And he seemed to be waiting for an answer. Very promising.

"I'm indigenous to the neighborhood. My mother even lives here."

"Nowhere to run, nowhere to hide."

"Aren't you going to ask me where I see myself in ten years? That's the topic that naturally follows how much the neighborhood has changed."

"I don't ask questions that I wouldn't want to answer," Patrick said.

"Something like "Don't ask questions on cross-examination when you don't know what the witness will answer.' "

"It's a variation on that theme."

"Good. I wasn't in the mood to discuss where I'll be in ten years."

"I'm never in the mood," Patrick said.

"Me either."

"So you're still living in the neighborhood and you're still practicing law." That other soul-mingling topic was coming up—how much people of any sensitivity hate being lawyers. Boy, they were hitting everything right on the nose today.

"Well, you gotta make a living," Nina said. That was the response that she had found most succinctly conveyed the fact that she was too highly evolved a human being for the money-grubbing practice of law but too cool to whine on and on about it.

They sat back and smiled at each other. Theirs were smiles of promise. They had successfully negotiated the preliminary round. They liked the way each other looked, they liked what each other had to say. Ten years ago the next move would have been to Nina's apartment. Being the way things were today, the next move was to check each other's schedule for the coming week.

"Are you going to be around this weekend?" Patrick asked. "I'd like you to meet my dog."

It was a cute line. It had a hint of intimacy without being threatening. Nina nodded. "I'd like to meet your dog," she said. With the right amount of feeling, she hoped. Enough to let him know that his rolled-up sleeves had turned her on. But not enough to make him think that she was an Upper West Side *desperada* that would follow him anywhere.

Then she remembered that was exactly what she was supposed to be. Someone who would schlep up a mountain with him and let him strangle her. She had momentarily forgotten about Susan and Williams and why she was here. Boy, this guy was good. He must be a hell of an investigator.

She tried to pull back and view him through Susan's eyes. He was the perfect combination of Cynical Intellectual and Real Man. Elite without being effete. It was a combination that rarely occurred in nature. Nina could tell that Susan would have liked him. She would have followed him anywhere.

"Maybe you can meet my dog on Saturday. If the weather's good, we can go on an outing."

"Sure. Do you hike?"

"Oh, yeah. I love to hike. Call me on Friday and

we'll check the weather report. You have my number, don't you?"

"I have your office number," Nina said.

"Office, home, car phone—it's all the same. You can always find me. I'm heavy into call forwarding. And I always carry this." He pulled out a beeper. Nina took it from him to examine it. As he took it back, he very briefly wrapped his hand around hers. "You can always find me," he repeated, elevating the words to rock lyrics in Nina's mind.

"That's good," she said, as she played with her hair.

# Chapter
# Seventeen

Patrick's dog was a redhead. A big, hefty mix of Irish setter and golden retriever. A good combination, actually. Not as thin and high-strung as most setters, the dog had the sturdy build and upbeat temperament of a retriever. But also had a beautifully colored auburn coat that looked great in the sun.

Patrick and his dog had parked at a hydrant in front of Nina's building and waited for her on the sidewalk in a patch of sunlight. As she emerged from her lobby, the dog came running up to her. She liked the animal instantly. There was something about it that made her want to drop to her knees and give it a hug. She settled for a few heartfelt pats on the head. "Great dog," she said.

Patrick gave her arm a squeeze. "It's good to see you," he said, looking directly into her eyes. The squeeze and the look were perfect, more intimate, yet less awkward, than a hello kiss.

"Nice day," said Nina, staring up at the sun. She

was having a hard time moving past two-word sentences. Patrick looked even better than the dog. She hadn't gotten much of a physical sense of him when he was hunched over at the tiny marble table in La Fortuna. But now she realized how wonderfully large he was. An old fashioned hunk, with broad shoulders and a thick neck and a small hint of a belly. Huggable, like his dog. He wore a forest green chamois shirt, rolled up again at the sleeves, tan corduroy pants and brown Rockport shoes with vibram soles.

Nina had worked hard and long to come up with her outfit. She wanted something devoid of any of the trendy Columbus Avenue characteristics that Patrick clearly detested, but still intelligently fashionable. And sexy.

She had rejected out of hand all of her jeans and flannel shirts. Grant, her former boyfriend, had found them sexy. But that was probably why she wasn't with him anymore. Then there was the feminized version of jeans and flannel shirts—all those long ethnic skirts and patterned sweaters she'd collected over the years. That Putamayo look was probably more up Patrick's alley, but those outfits precluded wearing running shoes. Since they were supposedly going on some sort of outing with the dog, Nina didn't want to be breathlessly clunking behind in cowboy boots. There was nothing less cool than a woman in inappropriate footwear. The perfect thing would have been something along Banana Republic lines—khaki pants, a big white shirt, and photojournalist's vest. It was a look Nina had always admired. But alas, she was doomed to admire it from afar. For, far from looking like Sigourney Weaver in *Gorillas in the Mist,* such outfits made her look like a chubby, middle-aged suburbanite in a safari suit. She had certain rules in life. One of them was, if they're pants, they're black. And twenty-seven different pockets on a vest did little to minimize bulk. Nina felt strongly that before a woman walked into Banana Republic, she should make sure that she was within six inches of Sigourney Weaver's height and within twenty pounds of her weight. Nina missed both standards. Not by a lot, mind you. But by enough.

She had settled on her black jumpsuit. It was clingy enough to be sexy, but plain enough not to be trendy. Actually, after mornings like these, routing through her closet for the perfect casual outfit, she always settled on her black jumpsuit, because her jumpsuit had something going for it that all those interesting ethnic outfits did not. It made her look thin. And despite decades of consciousness raising, that still gave it an irresistible appeal.

With the jumpsuit she wore black suede Reeboks and red socks for color. It was warm enough to carry her jacket. "Nice day," she said again.

"It's a gorgeous day. Feels like it's almost seventy." The dog jumped up against Patrick's hip. "This is Daisy," he said.

"A female?"

"Yup."

"Great name." Really, Nina scolded herself, since when are you incapable of stringing more than two words together? It was funny how years of careful training in overcompensating for shyness could suddenly evaporate. She pulled herself together. "So where are we off to today?"

"I don't know. We could go anywhere. Any preferences?"

"How about the Bronx Zoo?" Like her black jumpsuit, it was always Nina's preference. She particularly liked the small mammal house. Since childhood, when she would beg her parents to let her have a pet kangaroo rat or ring-tailed lemur.

"They won't let Daisy in there. Do you feel like taking a drive up to Bear Mountain?" he asked. "It would be a shame to waste a day like today."

"I can't get back too late. I'm due at my sister's house in Brooklyn by six." She wasn't really. Her sister and family would never have spent such a gorgeous weekend in the city. Laura was surely out at her house in the Hamptons, drying herbs and pickling things.

But Williams had absolutely forbidden her to go hiking with Patrick. "You can go out with him again," he had said, "but keep it urban. Someplace where there are people around." Where could you take a dog where there were people around? Where everyone else took their dog, she guessed—Central Park.

"Why don't we just go over to the park?" Nina said.

"Daisy doesn't consider Central Park to be outdoors. Too crowded." Nina felt a small tremor of fear. Was he trying to use his dog as a way to lure her to a deserted place? "But it's fine with me," he added. "I'm always up for people-watching. I don't get to do much of it up in Rockland."

Nina tried to calm herself down. See, she was being ridiculous. This guy wasn't trying to lure her anywhere. She should just have a good time. Specimens like Patrick did not walk into your life every day. And unfortunately one never knew when they were going to walk out again. Experience had taught Nina that if you don't relax and have a good time on the first three dates, you're missing something. Because after that it's usually downhill.

"I mean, there are plenty of people to look at up

there," he continued. "You can hang out at the Nanuet Mall and watch thousands go by. But they're not really worth watching."

"I know. How many hours can you spend looking at couples in acid-washed jeans and dopey sweatshirts? That's the thing about Manhattan. You can't park, you can't play tennis outdoors, you can't get into a movie without waiting in line, but it's really the only place where the people are worth watching." She felt contrived as she made her little speech, as if she were writing a magazine article. What was all this shit about outdoor tennis? The only competitive sport she actually indulged in was gossiping.

"Well, you certainly can't park. But we're going to have to try." He opened the back door of his Subaru wagon and Daisy jumped right in. As Nina opened the door to the passenger's side, he apologized for the condition of the car. "Sorry for the mess. I practically live in here." He pulled a pile of newspapers and file folders off her seat before she slid in and tossed them onto the floor in back.

"I've seen worse."

"Is that somebody pulling out back there?" he asked, looking into the rearview mirror.

Nina turned around. "Yeah, and it looks legal."

Patrick gracefully backed the car down the street and pulled into the newly vacated spot. He did it masterfully. In New York there are too many people who drive only in rented cars on occasional weekends. And they never seem to be truly at ease until Sunday night, when it's time to turn the thing back in. Nina, despite her summer as a cab driver, was rapidly turning into one of these cursing and sweating drivers. Patrick, on the other hand, was clearly an owner, not a renter.

They walked over to the park and entered at Seventy-second Street. Then they headed over to the Sheep Meadow. Patrick carried Daisy's tennis ball with him. She was glad he hadn't brought a frisbee for the dog. Those things should be confined to Southern California. Not that it really mattered anymore. These days the inability to windsurf was more of a worry than ineptitude with a frisbee.

There was a skateboard competition being held on the drive that ran along the west side of the Sheep Meadow. Young men in Lycra bicycle pants negoti- ated a set of difficult barriers. She caught herself ogling their well-muscled derrières. She had noticed a while ago that she was turning into an old letch, but she told herself that she was making up for lost time. When she was as old as the skateboarders were now, the most revealing outfit that she ever saw on a man was a pair of floppy denim cut-offs. And muscle definition had not yet been introduced to the middle class. In college, joint rolling was about as strenuous as it got. Besides, the idea back then was to be as skinny as possible. Since your parents were probably fat, it was your political duty to be thin. All she could remember from that period was a series of pale, reedy young men in BVD tee shirts and bell-bottomed jeans with flat rear ends. There hadn't been a buttock mus- cle among them. These days there was much more to look at. Nothing was flat. There were curves every- where—breasts, thighs, biceps, rear ends, even calves were rounder. It was as if the Great Creator had moved out of his Cubist period and into a Renoir phase. Maybe Nina would have been better off if she had come of age now. Then she had felt like a round peg in a square hole.

As Patrick ran ahead to separate Daisy from a vola- tile German shepherd, she checked out the rear view. He had a nice curve to his tush. Not as pronounced as the skateboarders, but nice. Nina wondered if he was a devoted Nautilus user. She would guess not. Maybe free weights. Or perhaps he just stayed in shape the old-fashioned way, the way guys used to back in the P.F. Flyer days—by playing basketball with their buddies on the weekend and giving the dog a run every now and then. He did have an old-fashioned pre-marathon body—thick, without bulging muscles. Casual bulk. Whatever it was, she like the broad contours of his body. Patrick, like her black jumpsuit, made her look thin.

Suddenly the thought of lying around the Sheep Meadow with him made her nervous. She might completely melt. She was already starting to ooze. "How about a game of miniature golf?" she suggested. "I hear that Trump has built a course on the Wollman rink. Or is it called the Trump Rink by now?"

"It probably is. I don't think they'd let Daisy in. But I'd be interested to see it sometime. I can just imagine what it looks like—Hole Number One would be Trump Tower, Number Two would be the Trump Shuttle terminal, Number Three would be the Trump Taj Mahal's casino, and so on."

"You're not a fan?" Nina asked.

"Well, I don't understand why the public is so fascinated by him. To me he's just another boring, narcissistic businessman. There's nothing cool about him. I mean, would you have gone out with him in high school?"

"Of course not. I like the more tortured, sensitive types. I still do."

"You do?" Patrick put a hand at the back of her waist. It was a large hand. It covered the whole space between the top of her belt an the bottom of her bra. It was large and warm. Hot, in fact. It burnt a hole right through to her stomach and sent a flush up her chest to her face.

"Tortured and sensitive. Is that you?" she asked, somewhat breathlessly, since she seemed incapable of maintaining normal body functions at the moment.

"Tortured? Definitely. But sensitive? I don't know. You'll have to tell me." His hand seemed to grow even bigger. What was happening? It was pushing her. Pulling her, really. Where? Towards him, of course. He was pulling her towards him and he was bending over. What was going on? She honestly didn't figure it out until she had been kissing him for what seemed like an hour. And by that time she had gone completely limp. No, limper than limp—liquid.

# Chapter
# Eighteen

Door Number Three had cancelled at the last minute, so Nina went over to her mother's instead. On her way into the apartment she did her usual refrigerator check, grabbed a yogurt, and continued on into the dining room. On the table sat a big bunch of white freesias in a crystal vase. "Nice flowers," Nina said to Ida. "Who gave them to you?"

"No one. I bought them."

"Are you having company?"

"No. No special occasion. I was just in the mood for some flowers." Nina looked at her mother questioningly. Ida just shrugged. "What's the big deal?"

"No big deal." Nina thought for a moment. "Except for four things."

"Okay." Ida sat down at the table. "I'm ready. Go ahead."

"Number one: For the past thirty-five years, I cannot remember a single time when you bought flowers just for the hell of it. Flowers are something you know you're going to end up throwing out. The thought of throwing anything out kills you. Look at your freezer, for Chrissakes. It's filled with microscopic bits of leftovers that you couldn't bear to part with." Nina thought back to their years in the Bronx. She was pretty sure that the only time there were flowers in the house was when they had gotten to take the centerpiece home from a bar mitzvah.

"Number Two: Freesias. I can't believe you actually bought freesias. You only get about four to a bunch. For the same four-ninety-nine, you could have gotten seven tulips or nine carnations or a dozen daisies."

"Daisies don't last as long," Ida protested weakly.

Nina nodded. "Good point, fair enough. But I don't really think of you as a freesia type. I mean, I never even heard of freesias until a couple of years ago. I'm sure they must have existed all along. Somebody must have known about them. But I can't remember ever seeing one until the eighties. Sort of like investment bankers."

"Yeah," said Ida. "When were investment bankers invented, anyway?"

"I don't know. Don't digress. Number Three," Nina continued. "There are about eight, ten stems in that vase. Which means that you must have bought more than one bunch. You actually pulled two bouquets out of the bucket, marched over to the cash register, handed the man a ten-dollar bill and didn't get any change. It's not like you. Are you having an affair?"

"From your mouth to God's ear."

"Okay, you're not wearing perfume or makeup or anything, so we'll rule out your having an affair. Number Four: These flowers are white."

"What's wrong with white? White is classic in its simplicity." Ida mocked Katharine Hepburn's accent.

"Exactly. I don't know how to put this in a way that won't offend you, but white flowers are not, um, terribly Jewish, if you know what I mean. You're a woman that has purple batik pillows on her couch and wears red Mexican shawls and big turquoise earrings. White has never been your color. Too subtle. White flowers are very Connecticut. As in White Flower Farms."

"What's White Flower Farms?"

At least Ida didn't know about White Flower Farms, Nina thought. Yet. "A fancy mail order garden business in Litchfield."

Now that she thought about it, it wasn't the first time she had had this sort of conversation with her mother. Once Ida had pulled a bag of figs out of the refrigerator. Nina was shocked. And recently, when she had admired one of her mother's blouses, Ida told her that she had bought it on Madison Avenue. Of course, she had bought it for fifteen dollars at a boutique that was going out of business. But what was Ida even doing on Madison Avenue to begin with? It was those women her mother had been hanging around with. Ever since she had moved to Manhattan, Ida had been running with a faster crowd.

"Nina, people change."

"Not me. Ask my shrink."

"Even you."

"Well, maybe. My earrings have gotten smaller over the years."

"How's the manhunt going, by the way?" Ida asked.

Nina pursed her lips. Partly because she couldn't decide how much information to reveal to her mother. And partly because if she didn't purse her lips, she would have broken into a big grin at the thought of Patrick. And that would never do. "Interesting," Nina said. "It's going . . . well, interestingly."

Ida smiled. "All right. You don't have to tell me anything if you don't want to. But I've been meaning to ask you about something."

"About what?"

"Motive."

"What do you mean?"

"Have you figured out why this man, whoever he is, killed Susan? I mean, I think it's important, don't you?"

"I guess he was crazy," Nina said.

"Well, he was clearly unbalanced in some way. He'd have to be, to commit such an act. But in my experience, even crazy people have motives."

"And how much experience with crazy people do you have?"

"Nina, I spent thirty years locked up in a classroom with thirty-five different children every year. You don't think some of them were nuts? Not to mention all those assistant principals I worked under. All crazy as loons."

"I guess I haven't focused on motive."

"I have a theory," Ida said.

"Why am I not surprised?"

"I don't know if you're aware of this, but Susan used to make me very angry. I used to want to throttle her."

"Well, that's how she was killed. Throttled to death. So what was it that pissed you off about her?"

"It's subtle. But I found her pushy. Persistently so."

"Please, Ma. This is a recurring theme with you. Everyone is trying to take advantage of your daughter Nina. Who's such a schlemiel that she can't look out for herself. Ever since 1959, when someone cut in front of me at the sliding pond line.''

"Susan was greedy," Ida said steadily. "She wanted things that other people had. And she would drive them crazy until they gave them to her.''

"You're still all bent out of shape because I gave her that silver pendant with the Eilat stone? Ma, that was twenty years ago. The thing must have cost Aunt Ethel a big five bucks. Three if she bothered to bargain. And anyway, I never used to wear it.''

"Yes, you did. You liked it. I remember how surprised you were that Aunt Ethel actually gave you something you liked. And Susan hocked you to death until you gave it to her.''

"Okay. Maybe Susan was a greedy little piglet and I was a sucker.''

"You were. Always waiting on street corners for her for hours. It used to make me so mad.''

"But she wasn't like that with men. She was overly deferential, if anything.''

"Maybe on the surface. But underneath I'm sure she was still Susan," Ida said.

"Maybe as far as the persistence goes. Susan was pretty obsessive. She'd go on and on and wouldn't let go. She was a tenacious little motherfucker.''

Her mother nodded. "That's what I meant. A tenacious little motherfucker.''

"But in terms of wanting things that other people had, I really think that was an issue she had with other women, not men.''

"Isn't it an issue you would have with people, not just men or women?''

"Mother, I understand that you're an old-time progressive that subscribes to the 'we are all one' line of thought. That there are no real differences between black and white or men and women. That we are all capable of doing the job. And I think it's very sweet. But that kind of antiquated egalitarianism isn't getting anyone anywhere anymore. It's a lovely sentiment that went out with nosegays and ice skating on frozen ponds."

"And it's been replaced by what?"

"Sexual politics," Nina said. "My theory is that there are two kinds of women: Women who want what men have—power, audacity, money; and women who want what other women have—protection, a husband, a husband's money. Susan was the second kind of woman."

"And you're the first kind of woman?"

Nina thought about it. "I'm sort of a hybrid. I want what whoever else is in the room has. Even if it's a cold."

"That's not really true. I don't think of you as an envious type of person."

"Not envious in the traditional sense. But I'm willing to question the validity of my existence at the drop of a hat. To decide that I should be doing what someone else does instead of what I do."

"That's insecurity."

"Yup. That's me. Classically insecure. All these new psychological categories that they've invented—narcissism and borderline personalities and all that. None of it fits me as well as that oversimplified stereotype that's been around since God-knows-when—the inferiority complex."

"Don't you think that your 'two kinds of woman model' is just as antiquated as my egalitarianism?" Ida asked.

"What do you mean?"

"According to the magazine articles, there's a whole new post-feminist generation out there. The younger ones, who take egalitarianism for granted."

"I'm not so sure I believe in post-feminism," Nina said.

"You don't believe it exists, or you don't believe it should?"

"I think it's just a stage these woman are going through. I'll admit that they feel exempt from sexism now. Remember, there are women already in the workplace that were educated at a co-ed Exeter and a co-ed Princeton. Not only were they educated at a co-ed Princeton, but they actually ate at co-ed Princeton eating clubs. They grew up playing soccer and were computer literate since puberty. And so far they've glided easily into prestige jobs and still claim that they want to have children before they're thirty. And they just give you a blank stare when you start talking sexual politics."

"You don't think it will last?"

"Of course not. They're in a youthful state of grace. Now, my generation went through the same thing. Not with sexism, which we all knew existed and were battling all the time, but with classism. We thought class distinctions were something that had plagued our parents' generation, but that we had successfully eliminated. We went to large state universities with a broad cross-section of students and hung out and smoked dope with anyone regardless of their background. We didn't know how much money someone's parents had. We even refused to acknowledge that any of us had parents."

Ida smiled. "How flattering."

"You know what I mean. Anyway, the whole thing came crashing down pretty hard. All of a sudden everyone's joined the same country club as their family. Except for people like me, whose parents belonged to the 92nd Street Y instead of a country club."

"I'm still a member. Are you?"

"No, I decided to stop torturing myself and stay out of that freezing swimming pool." Nina got up to toss out her empty yogurt container. "I have a prediction: Sexism will become moot," she said. "In this country anyway."

"How could it become moot?"

"We're headed for a two-class society. It'll be like South America, where a few very wealthy assholes will be able to do whatever they want, regardless of gender. And the rest of society will be struggling through life, too preoccupied to have the luxury of examining such issues."

"Now you sound like your father." Sometimes she did sound like her father. Leo Fischman had been a cerebral mix of bitter cynicism and a tiny residue of utopian socialism. He had not been a man who bought freesias.

Nina turned her attention back to Susan's murder. It was Ida's theory that Susan had wanted something from this man. Could Nina's best friend from high school have been a cold-blooded blackmailer? She doubted it. Although Nina did have to admit that she had never wanted to part with Aunt Ethel's Israeli necklace.

# Chapter
# Nineteen

It had been strange, calling up a fifty-five-year-old cop to tell him all about your date. It was definitely different from discussing men with Susan Gold. Williams asked an entirely different set of questions, for one thing. Nothing about what he wore and whether or not he was a good kisser. Williams confined his line of inquiry to trying to ferret out erratic behavior, something that Susan had never bothered to do until it was too late.

"I don't really think that Patrick exhibited anything that could be considered erratic behavior," Nina said in response to his questions. "But then, I can't always tell. I have low standards when it comes to that."

"Well, did you feel threatened in any way?" Williams continued.

"Look at who you're talking to. I feel threatened even when I'm sitting alone in a room. You don't expect me to get through an entire date without feeling threatened, do you? To me, it's like breathing."

Williams didn't laugh. "Try to cut through the shtick," he said seriously, "and figure out whether Patrick did anything that made you feel scared or worried about your well-being."

She thought about it. "No, not really. Actually, it was great. I had a wonderful time. I think he's a very nice man."

"Okay. But I still want you to proceed with some degree of caution. Did he mention hiking?"

"Well, when we were first deciding where to go, he did suggest Bear Mountain. But he didn't seem put out when I steered him away from it. And during the course of the afternoon, we discussed some upstate day trips we might take, including some hikes. But he didn't push anything."

"I'd like you to get to know him better before you let yourself get into a vulnerable situation, okay?"

"I think I'm already in a vulnerable situation."

"I meant physically vulnerable, not emotionally. The latter is up to you," Williams said. Then his voice softened a bit. "Nina, you should be aware that I can afford you physical protection only. If I could afford people protection from emotional vulnerability, I'd retire from the force tomorrow and open up an office in your neighborhood."

"Yeah, I know a lot of people I could give your card to." After a wistful pause, she changed the subject. "Can we cross that asshole architect off the list or do I have to go out with him again?"

"Victor Gibson? What do you think?"

"There's no way that Susan could ever have gotten involved with that guy. For one thing, he said he had never met anyone from the Bronx before," she said.

"If you had just murdered someone from the Bronx, what would you say?"

"But he also said he hardly ever goes hiking."

**139**

"If you had just murdered someone from the Bronx on a hiking trail, what would you say?"

"I can't exactly explain why, but I think we should cross him off the list."

"Is that because you don't think he's guilty, or because you can't stand the thought of going out with him again?"

Nina thought about it. Actually, she didn't really want to go out with any of the other men on the list that she and Williams had compiled so carefully. Patrick had definitely distracted her from this investigation. She had better rein herself back in. "I'll go out with him again if you think I should. But it would probably mean that I would have to do the calling. He certainly didn't seem interested in pursuing me."

"What did he say at the end of the date?"

"After lecturing me about various topics for an hour—ranging from single malt Scotch to the architectural integrity of Chicago's skyline—he said, sort of perfunctorily, 'I've enjoyed talking to you.' It was all I could do to stop myself from screaming 'don't you mean talking *at* me?'"

"And that was it?"

"Then he said, rather vaguely, 'perhaps we'll do this again sometime.' And I said 'okay' and he got out of the cab and I haven't heard from him since."

"Well, you can't possibly have been offended. You said you disliked him on sight."

"Since when does one thing have anything to do with the other?" Nina asked.

"You're telling me that even though you thought the guy was a pompous asshole, you're offended because he didn't ask you out again?"

"I guess it's like that old joke about that woman held captive by King Kong. She finally escapes, and then complains to her friend that he doesn't call, he doesn't write.''

"Unbelievable.'' Williams said.

"I went out and bought a leopard headband for the occasion. Seriously, it's very hard to get past thinking that the entire world should throw themselves at your feet, whether or not they happen to be assholes.''

"I'm finding that this investigation is developing some unanticipated pitfalls.'' He thought for a moment. "Nina, cut it out,'' he said sharply.

"What do you mean?''

"So far, we've set this thing up well. I don't want you to mess it up by indulging your neuroses. I want you to take it seriously.''

Once again it seemed to Nina that he had cut through to the core of the matter, by-passing years of therapy. Maybe all the cops in New York should switch jobs with the psychotherapists, and everyone would be better off. "Okay, I will,'' Nina said, meaning it.

"We'll keep Gibson on the inactive list; how's that?'' Williams said. "We'll summon him up again if we need him.''

"Fine with me. Whatever you think best.''

"Good attitude. Now, moving down the list, I have John DiMeo next. Have you made contact?''

"Oh, him.'' Nina didn't sound thrilled.

"I guess you have. What's wrong with DiMeo?''

"I had this very weird phone conversation with him. When he answered my ad, he described himself as a divorced businessman. It took me about two minutes of conversation to figure out that he's not really divorced and he's not really a businessman.''

"What is he?''

"He's somewhat separated. That is, his wife has him living in the basement of their house in Yonkers.

And he's somewhat of a businessman. He and his brother own a couple of taxi medallions. But what he really does is work for the New York City Sanitation Department."

"Collecting garbage?"

"You got it. He went on and on about how he almost has his twenty-five years in and after he retires he'll be able to carry out all the entrepreneurial schemes he's had to put on hold all these years."

"He sounds like he's having a major-league midlife crisis," Williams said.

"That's what it sounds like to me. I guess I'm finally at the age where I can stop dating overgrown juvenile delinquents and move on to the midlife crises."

"So did you make a date with the garbageman?"

"I couldn't bring myself to. Can't we put DiMeo on the inactive list along with Gibson? I really don't think Susan would have gotten so worked up about someone whose wife keeps him in the basement."

"From what you've described, she's gotten worked up about a lot worse. Didn't you tell me that she had a rather involved affair with someone who lived out of his glove compartment?"

"Living in a 1968 Volkswagen camper is a lot more glamorous than living in a Yonkers basement."

"All right. You can put DiMeo on hold for now."

"Thank you," Nina said. "You've done a mitzvah."

"Don't get all soppy on me. Who's next?"

"The next guy sounds like more of a possibility. In fact, I'm sort of looking forward to this one."

"I'm happy for you. What's his name?"

"Irwin Smolkowitz."

"You're looking forward to meeting Irwin Smolkowitz?"

"He sounded very interesting over the phone,

despite the name. He's South African. He's only been in New York for about a year."

"South African?"

"We didn't have a political discussion, but I assume he's at least somewhat of a liberal."

"Why do you assume that? Because he's a Jew?"

"No. Because he has a brother who's a journalist."

"That makes a lot of sense."

"You know what I mean." Nina had to admit that she had erred on this front before. When she had lived out West, whenever she saw anyone in a down vest, she had assumed they were progressive. But, just as often, they turned out to be active members of the National Rifle Association.

"You're just a sucker for an accent."

"Well, so was Susan," Nina said defensively.

"Okay, he's at least worth checking out. Did you make plans with him already?"

"Yup. We're having dinner tomorrow."

"The poor Italian garbageman gets crossed off the list, but the South African skips the 'let's meet for a drink' phase and gets bumped straight up to dinner."

"Look, there are some wonderful white South Africans. The guy could turn out to be a male Nadine Gordimer."

"What does he do for a living?"

"He works in his family's business."

"And what kind of business is that?"

"Um, gems I think," Nina said faintly.

"He's a South African who works in his family's gem business. And you think he's going to turn out to be a champion of human rights."

"All right, I'm delusional when it comes to men. I never said I wasn't." Nina wondered idly whether Patrick knew who Nadine Gordimer was. Maybe she'd sneak her into their next conversation just to see. But she really should find out if he wore contact lenses before she found out whether he had ever read anything by Nadine Gordimer.

"I hope you at least get a decent meal out of the guy," he said.

"I have a good shot at it. We're eating someplace where you have to order the dessert soufflés in advance."

"You mean that when you call in the reservations, you have to tell them what you want for dessert?"

"No, the way he explained it to me, when you order your entrée, you have to tell them whether or not you want a soufflé for dessert."

"That Irwin Smolkowitz. He's a real man about town, huh?"

"I guess I'll find out tomorrow." Somehow her conversation with Williams had taken some of the romance out of the idea of Irwin Smolkowitz.

# Chapter
# Twenty

Irwin Smolkowitz did not look like the son of a South African gem dealer. He looked more like a career postal employee who kept stacks of anarchist tracts in his locker. He wore a beat-up sport coat, and his wild graying hair and beard made him look like a painfully thin, stooped version of Jerry Garcia. He wore gold-rimmed glasses with a Band-Aid on the left earpiece. And he smelled, just the tiniest bit.

He certainly didn't look like the sort of person who ordered dessert soufflés in advance. Yet here he was, sitting at the charming country French bar of La Tulipe, reading the *Atlantic Monthly*. He was alone at the bar and Nina was a good ten minutes late, so there could be no mistake that this creature was Irwin Smolkowitz. By all rights, Nina's heart should have sunk. But instead of experiencing a "let me out of here" kind of revulsion, she felt her antennae go up, and a brisk "let's get to the bottom of this" feeling took over.

As she approached him, he became aware of her existence and stood up. He shifted the *Atlantic* to his left hand so that he could extend his right. This was done awkwardly and took longer than it should have. "Nina? Irwin Smolkowitz here. Nice to meet you." She loved colonial accents. They were British, yet weren't, almost like an American actor trying to imitate the King's English.

No need to even keep this guy on the inactive list, Nina thought as they approached the dining room. Lousy build, lousy haircut. No haircut, in fact. And no contact lenses. Yet there was something intriguing about Irwin Smolkowitz. He had a mystery all his own, even if it had nothing to do with Susan Gold.

The man who seated them seemed to be the owner. He looked more like a university professor than a restaurateur. And he addressed Irwin Smolkowitz by name. It was hard to tell if old Irwin was a regular or if the owner had just checked the reservations list, since he used an air of intimacy that had clearly been cultivated over years of restaurant ownership.

It was a small dining room, and the decorative scheme was calculated to make new diners burst into a chorus of "charming." For charming it was, there was no other way to describe it. It had brick and dried floral wreaths and fireplaces. And, of course, tulips on every table. Even if nothing else came of this series of dates, she was at least getting to see a lot of tulips.

"What do you think of the restaurant?" Irwin asked, as they settled into their seats.

Nina struggled for a less obvious adjective, but it was impossible. It was like trying to think about anything other than pink elephants. She gave up. "It's charming." She looked around. "Very charming," she said, getting into it.

"I like it," Irwin said with an air of propriety. Maybe he did come here often.

The waiter arrived with the menus, which were also charming. Oversized and written in script, they featured duck paired with lentils and other country French fare. What was even more charming was that all the dinners were *prix fixe*. Nine liked a place where you bought your ticket and you got your eats. No obsessing about whether or not to order an appetizer. Here the appetizers were a given. There was a small upcharge, however, for the blini with caviar. She decided to avoid that, since the menu advised that you accompany your blini with vodka and the whole thing seemed too complicated. She wasn't the kind of woman who could pull off ordering Absolut, very well chilled. She never knew whether or not to drop the *t* in the brand name and could never convey the requisite sense of urgency in the world *very* like other people seemed to. She decided on the sorrel soup instead. She had never tried sorrel soup before, but had read a recipe cautioning her to clean the sorrel well, otherwise the soup would be hairy. The notion of hairy soup was so compelling that she ordered it, half hoping she would get to see what that meant. Although she knew that in a place like this, they were likely to clean the sorrel thoroughly.

She couldn't decide between the duck and the veal. There was something appealing about pairing duck with lentils, certainly more appealing than pairing brown rice with lentils. Which was what she usually saw lentils hanging around with. She finally decided on the veal, her theory in life being that when veal crosses your path, you should take advantage of the situation. Although, these days veal seemed to be politically incorrect, an updated version of Gallo wine.

As the waiter approached, Irwin leaned across the table towards her. "I'm not having a drink before dinner," he whispered urgently. "Are you?"

"Oh, I guess not. Should we just have wine?" This guy was definitely weird.

"I don't drink. But you may order for yourself, if you like." Drinking was going the way of smoking, it seemed. It was only a matter of time before there would be just a few eccentrics left who actually made a habit of it. She could handle it, she supposed. She was halfway there herself, compared to the days when she could sit around all night, throwing back shots of tequila. But she would always hold on to her romantic notions about alcohol. Even smoking— which she had given up ages ago and was clearly a filthy and disgusting habit—still had an air of romance about it. Whenever she saw an old movie and watched Fred Astaire fondle a crystal martini pitcher or watched Simone Signoret turn a cigarette into an erotic object, she felt the loss. She tried to remind herself that not only was Simone Signoret dead, but sometime around 1970 she had begun to resemble Nina's grandmother. It was as if Signoret's Jewish half, which had lain dormant all those years while she ran around in full slips, smoking cigarettes, had suddenly popped out when she hit sixty. And Fred Astaire was also dead (although he seemed to have made it through life without being a homosexual, unlike most of the other romantic male leads who had fondled crystal martini pitchers on the screen) and no one smoked or drank much anymore. Including Irwin Smolkowitz.

What should she do now? She couldn't very well order a bottle of wine for herself. Jewish girls from the Bronx didn't do that. Think of the waste. And Nina somehow felt that this was too tony a joint for a glass of house white. She didn't know if the concept even existed in such a place. But she definitely needed a drink. She could not get through the evening by staring at Irwin Smolkowitz through only an Evian haze. "I'll have a glass of Lillet, please." A friend had taught her that trick. It was white wine, but not really. You didn't have to open a whole bottle just to get a glass. And she knew she was supposed to drop the "t" in Lillet.

She subjected Irwin to closer scrutiny. She could not, by any stretch of the imagination, describe his look as casual wealth. The guy looked like a bum. But he had to be loaded. It seemed to her that most out-of-town Jews were. It was not just the South Africans and Australians who were really rich. But even the American Jews who grew up in the Midwest or the South were likely to have at least a country club in their past. If Jews were from Cleveland, they were from Shaker Heights. If Jews were from Pittsburgh, they were from Squirrel Hill. It never failed. There were no Bronxes in these places.

Nina had a theory. It was that when everyone landed at Ellis Island, the ones with the initiative took off in their thread peddling wagons, or whatever. And the loxes stayed here, to breed in the vast tenements of New York City. And here she was, still living in a walk-up. A third-generation lox.

"So," Nina said, "you told me on the phone that you've only been living in New York for about a year. What do you think of it so far?"

"To tell you the truth, it reminds me of home." He sneered a bit.

"In what way?"

"I expected to find an integrated society. That's what we're led to think. Of course, we're not innocent enough to believe that your culture is devoid of racial problems. But nothing prepared me for what I found. The entire concept of an integrated society is a farce.'' He pulled on his hair with both hands as he spoke. ''In your offices I see large rooms of black people, filing and doing other menial tasks, while the whites are lined up along the windowed walls, one to an office. And all they seem to do is talk on the phone all day and give black people things to type. Blacks and whites often don't even use the same washrooms in these offices. And on your subways it's the same story. You see carloads of white people going home in one direction and carloads of blacks going home in another. Or if there's a mix on the train, all the white people get off the subway while it's still running as an express. Then it turns into a local and leaves the blacks on to slowly wind their way home to their unfashionable outlying districts.''

It was basically true. Except at the tip of each subway line, there was usually a quasi-suburban pocket that kept a few white passengers on to the bitter end. Riverdale, Howard Beach, Jamaica Estates, places like that. Nina decided to refrain from pointing this out. He didn't seem like the kind of guy that enjoyed being contradicted. ''I see you've been in the offices and the subway. Not leading too sheltered an existence, are you?''

''Did you think I spent all my time in places like this? Is that why you went out with me?''

''Not at all.''

''Disappointed, eh?'' There was clearly no way to prevent Irwin from getting hostile. Hostility was clearly his life. Should she bother to explain how she was not just another one of those white people that got off the train while it was still running express? Why bother. She reached for her Lillet and let him continue. ''Let me tell you something about New

York Jews," he said. "They're wearing blinders. The analogy is so clear and they just won't see it."

"What analogy is that?"

"To the German Jews, of course. Back when there were any. Jews in this city think that they own the place. That they've assimilated themselves into a position of power. This could be Frankfurt in the twenties. They're philanthropic, they hold elected office, and they intermarry. Have you ever been to services at Temple Emanu-El on Fifth Avenue?"

"Can't say that I have." Nina dived into her soup, which had just arrived. It was, as she expected, hairless.

"There's not a Jewish woman in the place."

"I think you may be mistaking cosmetic surgery for actual Christian blood," she said.

Irwin got a big kick out of that one. He laughed raucously, almost upsetting his appetizer, which was an austere mixed green salad. Then, just as suddenly, he stopped. "You can joke about it," he warned, leaning over his plate towards Nina, "but don't forget what happened to all those self-satisfied, quasi-Protestant German Jews."

"Do you see it coming here?"

"Don't you?" He stared at her, looking quite the madman. The wild hair, the shabby outfit, the mended glasses, and his glaring intensity all stood out in stark contrast to the pink tulips and dried floral wreaths.

Nina's impulse was to say something calming and reassuring. To cluck no, no, no, don't be silly, everything's going to be all right. But she wasn't much of a clucker. Besides, she had to admit to herself that Irwin's theory had previously occurred to her on occasion. She was, after all, her father's daughter. "Maybe," she said. Best to remain noncommittal. If she enraged this guy, he might very well start flinging his watercress against the charming brick walls.

"There's no maybe about it." At that moment he looked capable of strangling her.

Nina was not used to being a good date. She knew she was capable of being a good listener. She could listen to her friends whine for hours. But listening to men and drawing them out and making them feel good had always seemed unprogressive. But now she told herself to put all that away and pull out all the stops. Being a Cosmo girl was becoming a matter of survival here. "You've given a lot of thought to some very interesting issues," she cooed. Or did a reasonable facsimile of cooing. "Did you ever think of becoming a journalist?"

"I told you, my brother is the journalist in the family." He was still scowling, but seemed to be softening.

"But don't you feel that all this creativity is being wasted, working in the family business?" His working in the family gem business actually made some sense, she realized. Irwin was the kind of son that made it worth your while to set up a New York office just to get him the hell out of his home town. Especially if his hometown was Johannesburg.

"Actually, I am working on a book." His voice had dropped to a more intimate decibel level. "Would you be interested in seeing it?"

She now saw how the evening would go. She would continue to act like the perfect date, an act she could sustain only with stark, raving lunatics. And he would eat it up and pester her forever. This had happened to her before. The question was whether this stark, raving lunatic was the stark, raving lunatic that she and Williams were looking for. Everything about him pointed to no. He wasn't what Susan had described, and certainly wasn't someone Susan would normally bother with. But maybe Susan had really been fed up. Sick of the men who said things like "sorry, I've been out of town for a month. I guess I should have told you I was going." Maybe Susan had been ready to pack it all in for a fabulously wealthy gem dealer who was too ugly and smelly to cheat on her. And maybe she had described him as attractive out of embarrassment. It was possible, Nina supposed. One thing was certain, however: If she was going to go off on a hiking trail with this creature, she was going to be damned sure to keep Detective James Williams within at least twenty yards of her at all times.

# Chapter
# Twenty-one

When Nina got to the office the next morning, she felt her usual surge of adrenaline. No matter how disgusted with her career she was at the moment, it always seemed like the office was where almost everything happened. It usually was the only arena she could rely on, day in and day out, for action. And she didn't seem to be unique. America had become a nation of people who lived their daily dramas in offices and then went home, turned on the television and watched fictional people live their daily dramas in fictional offices.

Today Nina's daily drama included a large, mysteriously shaped package that was waiting for her on the receptionist's desk. A messenger had just delivered it, the receptionist told her. Nina carried it into her office with her. There was a card taped to the top of the box. She opened the envelope, which contained a piece of Irwin Smolkowitz's personal stationery. "Since we didn't get to have breakfast together . . ."

it said. Nina looked at the box suspiciously. Irwin had been hard to get rid of last night. He had wanted to show her his apartment, he had wanted her to show him her apartment, he had wanted them to watch the sunrise from the Staten Island ferry. And on and on. She had finally gotten into a cab and left him on the sidewalk, still suggesting. He didn't seem like the type to send a letter bomb, she told herself. But that wasn't quite true. Actually, he seemed exactly the type to send a letter bomb.

She plunged in and removed the brown paper that covered what turned out to be a cake box. Inside the box was cream cheese and lox on a bagel. How sweet, Nina thought. How romantic. How Jewish. Too bad Irwin Smolkowitz wasn't somebody else.

What really impressed her was his ability to track down the address of her office. She had mentioned only once that she was a staff attorney with a legal services organization that assisted the elderly. He must have spent a good bit of time with the Manhattan directory to figure out where to deliver breakfast. Most impressive of all, however, was the fact that he had been listening to what she said.

It was the real way to a woman's heart, yet not many men seemed to know that. Or maybe they did, but still considered it too big a pain to bother. They built up their muscles, dropped big bucks on flashy cars and lately had been rubbing expensive—and potentially dangerous—chemicals into their scalps. When all they really had to do was listen. And remember.

There had been a man in her college dorm who hadn't looked much better than Irwin Smolkowitz. Yet he had, in the vernacular of the day, gotten laid a lot. Other men could never figure out his secret, but the women all knew. He was the only man Nina had ever met who, months after a casual conversation, could refer back to a minor something you said. Women did it to each other all the time, of course. But when a man did it, well, that was really something. She remembered being breathlessly awed by his ability. She had never actually slept with him, however. There had been too long a line.

Susan had known what she meant. Maybe Irwin had managed to mesmerize her with his memory. But it was hard to believe that at the end of Susan's long line of sexy samba dancers and rugged cabinetmakers and lithe yoga instructors could stand Irwin Smolkowitz. She wished Gwen were back from Europe. Despite Gwen's stormy relationship with Susan, Gwen was always astute when it came to Susan's men. She seemed to know how long they'd stick around and which would give her real trouble. Susan used to rely on Gwen as a sexual astrologer, calling her for a diagnosis of each new love interest. Gwen had been gone almost a month. She was due back soon, but one never knew. Gwen's new husband had mysterious overseas business, so she'd been vague about her itinerary and her return date.

Nina tried to pretend to be Gwen diagnosing Irwin Smolkowitz. She struck a Gwen-like posture, hand on hip and lips judgmentally pursed. She squinted at a mental image of Irwin Smolkowitz. "Yech," she said to herself, in Gwen's throaty voice. "Get him out of here."

Maybe Williams would have something helpful to say. Later in the day, when she finally got him on the phone and had described last night's and this morning's meals, she asked him what to do.

"Nothing much for you to do," he said. "Just sit tight."

"Should I call Smolkowitz and thank him for the

bagel? I mean, if you think he's a viable suspect, we shouldn't let him slip away."

"You think this guy is going to slip away? Nina, Irwin Smolkowitz is going to hound you to your grave. I can tell, you're not going to get rid of him so easily."

Williams made her feel like a rank amateur. Not only in detecting, but in dating. Which was why Susan used to use Gwen as her sexual astrologer instead of Nina. Nina, who prided herself in predicting the plots of everyday life, was always being taken completely by surprise in her involvements with men. She pictured a cartoon captioned "Nina and Men." There she'd be in her black jumpsuit with her eyebrows up in the air and her mouth round with shock. "Oh," she'd be saying.

"Well, do you think there's a possibility that he's guilty?" she asked Williams.

"I suppose so. Even if Susan hadn't encouraged him, if he had become obsessed with her, he might have followed her that weekend. We've been proceeding along the theory that whoever she was dating was the murderer. But we should remember that someone else could have trailed her and lured her into the woods in order to kill her. So the fact that Irwin Smolkowitz is too ugly and weird for either you or Susan to bother with doesn't necessarily rule him out."

"I hadn't thought of that. But that makes the whole thing so unbearably complicated."

"I'm sorry," he said in a way that made her aware that she was beginning to whine.

"All right. I'll just follow Irwin's lead, is that the best thing to do?"

"I'd say so. By the way, how long has it been since you sent in your answers to those ads?"

"Two weeks."

"Any calls yet?"

"Nothing."

"I'm not surprised," Williams said. "When you were drafting those replies, I thought it might lead somewhere. Or at least you'd get some interesting phone calls. But I've spoken to quite a few women since then, and they all tell me the same thing."

"What's that?"

"Basically that when a woman places an ad, she usually gets quite a few responses and feels like the belle of the ball. But when a man places an ad, he often gets hundreds of responses. So when you're answering an ad, even if you send a really great letter, there's still a good chance that the man will never get around to calling you."

"That makes me feel terrific."

"Or if he does call you, it will be after quite a few weeks have gone by."

"Since he's been busy sorting through hundreds of clever, witty letters from thirty-five-year-old, single, female Jewish lawyers. Maybe I should marry Irwin Smolkowitz."

"I don't think you should marry Irwin Smolkowitz. But for the sake of this investigation, you might want to answer his phone calls. You can be evasive, but don't dump him altogether. He's worth checking out further."

"Okay. Listen, do I have your permission to spend the night with Patrick Brennan? I want to find out if he wears contact lenses."

"Can't you just ask him?"

"He might lie."

"It makes me a little nervous," Williams said.

"It makes me a little nervous, too. But that doesn't seem to be stopping me."

"I'll tell you what. I'll send a patrolman over to hang out across the street. We'll give him a key. If you get into any trouble, flick the lights once and he'll come right up."

"Sounds useful. Can you do that for me for the rest of my life?"

"Why, do you intend to be dating for the rest of your life?"

"One never knows."

"That's true. Look at me," Williams said.

That shut her up. It was helpful, she had decided, when one started to feel sorry for oneself, to have an equally troubled—or more troubled—person nearby, conducting him or herself with tremendous dignity.

"When are you seeing Brennan again?"

"Friday night."

"And you're sure he'll be spending the night?"

"I have no idea. But it's a possibility." It wasn't really true that she had no idea. Dating was often like reading a novel. On some subconscious level, you knew what was going to happen next. But not always. Sometimes dating was like reading an O. Henry short story. The surprise ending could knock the wind out of you.

"Okay. If it turns out that you are going to spend the night together, make sure it's at your place, so we can keep an eye on him. And don't worry about Irwin. He's probably harmless."

"Let's hope probably is good enough," she said. But her mind had already drifted away from Irwin.

# Chapter
# Twenty-two

This time Patrick had left the dog home. Nina couldn't tell what that meant. It could mean that he'd have to leave early to go home and take care of her. But she preferred to think that Daisy was snug in her doghouse, leaving Patrick free to see what might happen.

As she climbed into his car, which was still a mess, she noticed a green nylon duffel bag on the back seat. He didn't seem like the kind of guy who packed his blow dryer every time he thought he might spend the night away from home. "Taking a trip?" she asked, pointing.

"That's my gym bag. I always keep it in the car, since I never know when I'll get the chance to work out."

"It wasn't there last time." Sometimes Nina's desire to know it all interfered with her ability to set a romantic mood.

"Maybe the stuff was in the wash. I do wash it sometimes." He sounded a little intruded upon.

"Oh." She tried to put a soft, seductive quality into the syllable, but she had a feeling that the damage was done. It was clearly a bad idea to cross-examine on the third date.

"Listen," he said, "I've got to drop something off at a friend's bar over on Ninth Avenue. How about we have a drink with him and then decide about dinner?"

"Fine." They headed east to Columbus, turned right and headed down past the point where the street dropped its pretensions and became Ninth Avenue. Patrick spotted a parking space near Fifty-second Street and pulled in.

Nina never felt comfortable in this neighborhood. Not because it was particularly dangerous, but because it didn't seem like New York to her. Formerly Hell's Kitchen, now rechristened Clinton, it was only half-gentrified. The housing stock still contained a lot of rent-regulated walk-up tenements, and its proximity to the theater district made it appealing to all the aspiring actors that still flocked to New York every year. They kept coming, despite everything. They seemed to pay no attention to the fact that the theater was dead and that only rich people could afford to live in Manhattan anymore.

The youngness and blondness of this group dominated the streets. Ninth and Tenth Avenues had more than their share of Mexican restaurants. Not that Nina disliked Mexican food, but it wasn't really something New Yorkers gravitated to. It had an out-of-town quality to it. While the rest of the country went wild over steak fajitas, New Yorkers tended to stick to Thai or Indian. Or, for the old-fashioned crowd, the ubiquitous Chinese. In Nina's mind, these Mexican restaurants were filled with Californian or Midwestern twenty-three-year-olds with small, regular features and long femurs, and enthusiasm in their voices. They pronounced all their *r*'s and wore blue jeans and pink sweatshirts instead of black. They made her feel old and thick and grumpy. And Jewish.

One could argue, of course, that Columbus Avenue had gone the same route. Certainly, it had its share of blondes and Mexican restaurants. But to the discerning eye, there was a difference. Further up, even in the West Sixties, but even more so in the Seventies, Eighties, and Nineties, there was still a vestige of a middle-class, middle-aged ethnic population. In any Empire Szechuan north of Columbus Circle, you could still see a man that looked like Philip Roth sitting with his mother or an original issue wife. There were enough people up there sprouting ear and nose hair to make Nina feel comfortable.

Patrick's friend's bar was basically an old-time tavern that had been spruced up with a few retro touches. It had black and white linoleum tiles and bar stools that swivelled, as if to announce "it's okay to drink here if you're young and trendy." The crowd was a mix: Some old timers that looked like they'd been glued to the spot since their discharge after the Korean War; some young blondes drinking margaritas; a table of ballet dancers, smoking cigarettes and drinking Diet Cokes. And a cluster of youngish blue-collar men at the bar who looked good enough to be an engine company of the fire department.

The music, which filled the place, was exactly the kind of music that hit Nina the hardest. Rock and roll from her pre-adolescence. The years she spent with Cousin Brucie, before she had felt compelled to move on to socially significant lyrics. The brief period when she actually bought 45s and walked around with a transistor radio. When people still used the word *teenager,* and it had a romantic excitement like nothing else. This was when teenagers still greased their hair back or wore rollers in the street. She had wanted so badly to be one. It was perhaps the last time in her life when Nina knew exactly what she wanted to be.

She had memorized every word of every song, from the bubble-gummy Lesley Gore white-girl stuff to the more compelling sounds of Motown. And to hear the music now always seemed painful. It some-how forced her to compare her present life to the deep longings and wild expectations she had had back then. Which always led to the question, "what have you become?" And Nina would have to look at her-self with her briefcase and dry cleaning and umbrella and dissatisfactions and face the answer. Which was "someone you didn't think you would become." And she would picture the eleven-year-old Nina, catching a glimpse into the future of the thirty-five-year-old Nina, being filled with shock and disappointment. Actually, what she really pictured was the eleven-year-old throwing her transistor radio out the window and jumping after it. So, even though she loved the music of that period, it had a beat you could dance to and it made her feel like moving; it also made her somewhat suicidal.

Trying to ignore any such impulses, she gave a warm hello to Patrick's friend Jim, who was behind the bar. He winked at her as he shook her hand. The wink wasn't exactly sleazy, but there was something calculated about it, as if greeting women were part of what he did for a living. Jim had one of those Eurotrash ponytails that Nina was still having a hard time getting used to.

He gave Patrick an affectionate punch on his right shoulder. "So how's the trickster?" Jim asked. Nina hoped it was a play on Patrick's name, and not his character.

"Can't complain," Patrick said. Nina always thought it odd when someone used that expression, since she could never say it with a straight face. If there was one thing she could always do, it was complain. "I've got your lease." Patrick handed Jim a file he had extracted from the rubble in his car. "Jim's one of my few remaining legal clients," he said to Nina.

"The man threw away a brilliant career," Jim said. "There was a time that you could walk through the halls of Criminal Court with him and the defendants would flock. Once, some guy came over to us and showed us a stack of dozens of business cards. He had kept the card of every lawyer who had ever represented him, both Legal Aid and private. The cards were rated, with stars on the back. He pulled Patrick's out and showed us five stars. Five was the highest."

"You call that a brilliant career?" Patrick said. "Five stars from some scumbag?"

"You were good," Jim said. "And you gave it all up so that you could drive around all day, hoping to get into a car chase."

"I don't drive around all day. That's not what I do," he said to Nina.

"What would you like to drink?" Jim asked her, smiling in the same professional way he had winked.

Nina could tell she wouldn't have the Irwin Smolkowitz Evian problem with this bunch. "I'll have a beer," she said.

"How about a Corona?" Her theory about the West Fifties and Mexican food had been right.

"What's that, some trendy new piss you're selling to the kids?" Patrick asked.

"I'll get you a couple of Heinekens, okay?"

"That's better." As Jim travelled down the bar to get the beers, Patrick tucked a piece of Nina's hair behind her ear. She smiled up at him, and he raised first his chin, then his eyebrows at her. The evening was starting to seem promising.

As Jim poured, Patrick's left thigh bumped up against Nina's right hip and stayed there. "Where are you two off to this evening?" Jim asked.

"Depends. What do you feel like eating?" Patrick asked her.

She thought she was best off shrugging, since she wasn't sure she could speak.

"There's a good neighborhood Italian place on the corner of Fifty-sixth," Jim said. "Nothing fancy. Garlic bread, red-and-white tablecloths, cheap Chianti."

"The way Italian restaurants are supposed to be."

"Yup. A real dinosaur."

"Sounds good," Patrick said. "Or we could go down to the Village if you want. We've got the car. We could go anywhere. What do you think?"

The record changed on the jukebox. The Mamas and the Papas started to sing "Go Where You Wanna Go." Cass Elliot was dead, but Nina was still alive. Was it too late to be someone you had thought you might become? "Or we could get take-out," she said turning to him.

He cupped her chin in his hand. "Yes," he said, "we could get take-out."

Jim leaned against the bar, watching and smiling. "In certain situations," he said, "take-out is definitely the best thing."

# Chapter
# Twenty-three

There was a police car parked on her block, with no one in it. But in front of Nina's building, leaning against a black Honda, was a man cleaning his nails with one of his keys. She saw him glance up at her window as she and Patrick turned into the front door, as if to give her some sort of high sign. He was either the patrolman that Williams had sent or else a very nosy vagrant.

Whichever he was, Nina had other things to worry about. Her underwear, for example. Under her sedate black slacks she was wearing a pair of pink satin tap pants that she had found in a thrift shop. At least, the woman in the store had called them tap pants, but Nina harbored a suspicion that they looked more like boxer shorts on her. She had bought them because they had the loveliest little pearl buttons and an interesting scalloped hem. But there remained the strong possibility that the scalloped hem hit her thigh in a bad place. Maybe she should plan on getting undressed in bed, where she wouldn't have to worry about it. Assuming, of course, she was going to be afforded the opportunity to undress. But then, what was the point of wearing antique satin tap pants with pearl buttons unless someone else was going to undo the buttons and let the tap pants casually drop to the floor?

And then of course there had been the inevitable issue of whether or not to wear pantyhose under the tap pants. Nina's legs definitely looked better in pantyhose, almost everyone's did. But then, what was the point of letting your tap pants drop casually to the floor if you had to then start pulling off your pantyhose? She had opted for the pantyhose anyway, since the alternative would have been socks, which really would look terrible with tap pants. And in the heat of the moment she might forget to take her socks off first.

She tried to calm herself down and stop thinking about her underwear, but the trip up her four flights of stairs was always unnerving. The stairs were too narrow for more than one person, so Nina had to ascend knowing that her rump was directly in Patrick's face. Which started her thinking about the hem of her tap pants again. By the time he folded his large frame into her undersized couch, she was pretty nervous.

"What can I get you to drink?" she said, still standing. "I have some beer that's cold, but I think it's Amstel Light. And I have some Jameson . . ." she trailed off, wondering if offering him Jameson was like someone offering her Manischewitz.

"A shot of Jameson would be nice." He didn't seem to be offended.

She opened the kitchen cabinet that served as her bar and took down the bottle. Conveniently, her kitchen was located in her living room. Maybe she should offer him ice. She racked her brain, trying to remember whether people put ice into Jameson Irish whiskey. She decided to err on the side of caution and skip the ice. She pulled two tumblers out of the dish drain, set the whole thing up on the coffee table and poured what she knew was too much whiskey into both glasses. Maybe three ounces of Jameson would get her brain to stop trying to jump out of her skull.

"Cheers," she said and threw about an ounce down her throat. Patrick just watched, amused.

"You seem a little nervous," he said.

"Yeah, well, here we are, you know."

"Yeah, here we are." He smiled.

She stifled an impulse to jump up and retrieve the Chinese take-out menu from the kitchen. It would just be, what they called in the theater, "a piece of business." She'd be better off sticking it out and concentrating on the plot.

"I'm glad," she ventured in a small voice.

"About what?" he asked.

"That we're . . . you know . . . here."

"So am I." He reached out and caressed the back of her neck. Nina had a sudden image of Susan's neck, bruised and broken. But the image disappeared as Patrick slowly worked his way into a shoulder massage. Nina felt herself opening up. That was how she felt, that everything was opening wider. Her eyes, her mouth, her legs. "Do you want me to rub your back?" he asked.

She didn't really want him to rub her back. Her back was playing a minor role in all this. Her front, now *that* was where it was happening. "Okay," she said anyway. What was she going to say, no? She didn't want to seem rude.

"Lie down," he said, his large hands guiding her face down onto the couch. She let her shoes drop to the floor. It was a good thing she had already worn her black jumpsuit on their latest date. Because if she had been wearing it now, Patrick would not have been able to slide his hands up under her blouse.

Her nipples felt like they were drilling holes into the couch. He was good, not only because he gave a good back rub, but because he seemed to be able to tell exactly when Nina started to feel that she couldn't stand it any more. And at that moment, he put his hands on her hips and gently turned her over. His face hung over hers as he outlined her lips with his finger.

"You have a beautiful mouth," he said, and kissed her gently and briefly. "And a beautiful neck," he said as he traced her collarbone. His lips rested there softly for a moment, and then he lifted his head and stared solemnly into her eyes. His right hand undid her top button. "May I?" he asked. She nodded.

He undid the rest of her buttons and opened her blouse. She was wearing a sheer bra, and they both looked down at her erect nipples. Patrick put his hand over one breast and kissed her lips, again briefly. Suddenly he pulled her up from the couch. "I want to look at you," he said, and stood her in the middle of the room.

He stepped back and just looked at her for a few moments, as if he were an artist and she were his model. Then he removed her blouse and laid it on the couch. He came back and knelt beside her as he unbuttoned and unzipped her pants. He pulled them down slowly and let Nina kick them off. "What do you call these?'' he said, sliding a hand up past the pink satin scalloped hem and cupping her ass.

"Tap pants," she said.

"Of course, tap pants. I like them. Sexiest tap pants I've ever seen," he said as he started on the lovely little pearl buttons. Then they both watched as the tap pants fell casually to the floor.

# Chapter
# Twenty-four

As Nina struggled to wake up the next morning, the first thought she had was that there was a man in her bed. She couldn't quite remember who it was, but she knew that she was glad he was there. A split second later, of course, she remembered everything. But that first moment of consciousness—when one is equipped with no facts, only feelings—is telling. And Nina was glad that she had felt the right thing.

"No contact lenses" was the next thought she had, as she watched Patrick still sleeping. That was encouraging. He had neither worn contact lenses nor attempted to strangle her last night. Both were good signs.

The next thing she realized was that she was starving. The only thing she had had for dinner last night was a shot of Jameson, and she hadn't even gotten to finish that. Fortunately, she had stocked up on breakfast food in case Friday evening were to turn out as successful as it had.

Sometimes she wondered if the guys in the deli on the corner could tell what was going on. Nina could. She could look at a woman at the cash register on a Friday night and know where her weekend was headed. It was the cream cheese that gave it away. The other stuff—the bagels, the orange juice, even the half and half—those were things that some women kept around for their own use. But when a woman brought an eight-ounce bar of Philadelphia Cream Cheese to the register, you knew she was expecting an overnight guest. The modern woman did not eat cream cheese except in the company of men. Sometimes Nina thought it would be less fattening to be celibate.

It was probably around ten, judging by the amount of sun in the room. Nina's apartment got about an hour of sunlight every morning. Good for growing African violets, but not much else, since it was an hour she rarely spent at home. She got up on an elbow to look at the clock, and Patrick stirred. He reached over and pulled her to him. "What's on the agenda?" he asked.

"We have an open agenda," she said. Mornings after were either terrible or wonderful, so she watched him carefully.

"I can think of two items of business," he said. "One of them is breakfast."

"Breakfast is definitely on the agenda. We've skipped enough meals as far as I'm concerned. Should I put the kettle on?"

"Put the kettle on," he said, then turned her face toward his and kissed her. "Put the kettle on later," he said.

An hour went by before Nina finally dragged herself out of bed to put on the kettle. That was the great thing about third dates, she thought as she stood in the kitchen, wearing her best bathrobe—more sex than talk. After that, things usually shifted to more talk about sex than sex, and then, eventually, you stopped even talking about it.

She peeled the foil wrapper off the cream cheese and put it into her special cream cheese dish. Since most of what she served to company seemed to be cream cheese, a large percentage of her china budget had been allocated for a porcelain Victorian cheese server. The rest of her dinnerware was less impressive, consisting mostly of what was left of what she inherited when Aunt Pauline had gone into the nursing home ten years ago.

Their clothes were still lying all over the floor of the living room. She left them there, forming a provocative little tableau. Patrick came into the room, wearing his briefs. He gave her a slap on the tush like he had known her forever.

"Smells great. Not decaf, I hope."

She handed him a mug of coffee. "Nope, it's the real thing."

He drank some. "It's good," he said and put his coffee down on the one square foot of counter space that Nina's kitchen contained. "I have something for you." He walked over and picked his jacket up off the floor. He pulled a gift-wrapped box out of the pocket. "I forgot to give it to you last night."

"Yeah, sure. You just wanted to see if you were going to get laid before you started showering me with presents."

"You know I'm not that kind of guy. I just got distracted last night. You're distracting." He held the box out to her.

It was about the size of a travelling alarm clock and wrapped in the kind of exquisite paper that you can buy only in individual sheets. This guy was too good to be true. An old-fashioned male virility that included working parts *and* sophisticated taste in wrapping paper.

In the box was a bottle of perfume. She took it out of the box. It was a spray bottle of frosted glass that contained a scent called Calyx. "Try some," he said, taking the bottle and giving her wrist a spritz. "Do you like it?"

She took a whiff. It was very citrusy and light. Sort of athletic. A jock perfume. It was nice. Nina was inexperienced when it came to scents. She used whatever relatives had given her for birthdays. She never had actually walked up to a fragrance counter and purchased anything. "I like it," she said.

"Would you wear it for me? From now on?"

"Sure."

"It's the only scent I can stand."

Nina got a little worried. It was the first time he had exhibited any of that "what kind of mushrooms are in the salad?"-type behavior that she so loathed. Maybe he was just another control freak in free spirit's clothing. What had she been wearing last night? She currently had bottles of Chloe and Opium working. She couldn't remember which she had used. He must have really hated whichever it was. And she had thought they were both socially acceptable scents. Her defensiveness faded away, however, as Patrick held her wrist close to his face and said, "Besides, it turns me on."

"Then, I'll wear it." She loosened her robe and let it slide down off one shoulder. She sprayed her neck and shoulder with the Calyx.

"Thank you," he said, sniffing and then nuzzling her neck. Now she understood what weak in the knees meant. She'd spray herself with anything this guy wanted. She'd put his favorite kind of mushrooms in the salad, even the ones that cost twelve dollars a pound, because feeling like this was something that didn't happen often. She was sure that in some lives it didn't happen at all. And she was hell-bent on enjoying it. Now, if only she could beat back that invisible, yet strong, undertow of worry that kept her wondering when all this was going to go away.

# Chapter
# Twenty-five

It was Williams on the phone. "There's a matter of some delicacy I have to ask you about," he told Nina.

Delicacy was such a funny word. For Nina, it never failed to conjure up images of tiny mounds of black caviar nestled in a bed of chopped egg. So it was always a disappointment when people, claiming to want to discuss a matter of some delicacy, ended up going on and on about money or sex instead of food.

Nevertheless, Nina's ears perked up when she heard the phrase. Anything out of the ordinary was something to look forward to. As well as loathe and fear, of course. Besides, there was something . . . well, delicious about matters of great delicacy. "Yes?" she said, waiting.

"Susan's gotten some unexpected mail," Williams said. "It's a seven-hundred-dollar bill from an anaesthesiologist for general anaesthesia during a surgical procedure that took place two weeks before her death. Do you know anything about this?"

"Surgery? How could she have had surgery? I don't even remember her missing a class at the gym."

"It took place on a Friday. An elective termination of pregnancy."

"Holy shit. Another abortion. She didn't say a word to me."

"So you had no idea she was pregnant?"

"Well, that's not exactly true. She called me one night to obsess about her period being late. But she was only a couple of days late. And when I asked her about it later, she said it was moot. So I just assumed she had finally started menstruating." Nina had lost the bead on that one. Well, there was a lot to keep up with. Parents of young children thought single people led carefree existences. They should only know. It seemed to Nina that getting married and having children was an excuse to limit your concerns to a mere three or four people. Being single meant that the sky was the limit. For one thing, you had all of your friends' menstrual cycles to keep track of. Not to mention having to keep more careful track of your own.

Although, the truth was that no one kept closer track of her menstrual cycle than a thirty-five-year-old married woman trying to conceive. The thermometers, the kits, the intense scrutinization of the texture of their vaginal mucus. Life was a cruel joke, really. First you spent fifteen or twenty years praying that you weren't pregnant, searching desperately for the tiniest speck of blood on the toilet paper. Then you decided to embark on the quest for conception and did a 180-degree turn. That same speck would make your heart sink, make you abandon all hope, doom you to another twenty-eight days of prayer and meditation. And fasting. Since this quest required an abstemious avoidance of caffeine, alcohol, tobacco, and even headache medication. That tiny speck of blood meant that your past four weeks of sobriety and caffeine-withdrawal headaches had been pointless. And that you were doomed to another potentially pointless month of the same. And there you were, back to calling it *the curse* again.

So Nina spent half her time listening to her single friends express their dread of skipping their period and her married friends express their dread of getting it. Actually, all this stuff wasn't so terribly new. Even back in the days when everyone wore overalls and entertained no notions of parenthood, they were all running around busily with their flashlights and mirrors and speculums getting acquainted with their cervixes.

"Did she say anything to you about the identity of the father?" Williams asked.

Nina tried hard to remember. She recalled Susan saying "Unclear, as always." But Nina couldn't remember what the question had been. Had she come right out and asked Susan who the father was? Or had she asked her whether he would stick around. Or maybe she had asked her what she was going to do about it.

"She didn't really say. And I didn't push it. She was sexually active, you know. And it never seemed prudent to keep track of how sexually active. Anyway, I really don't know if he was the same guy she went hiking with. I'm pretty sure the late period occurred before she even mentioned this guy to me, so maybe it wasn't his child. Or maybe she didn't know who the father was. She'd been known to change partners pretty rapidly. Sometimes there was some overlap."

"She kept a pretty full dance card, I take it?"

"Yes, she did. Of course, she went through periods of abstinence like anyone else, when she'd decide to give it all up. But they never lasted long. Never longer than your typical crash diet. Celibacy was mostly a Monday morning thing with Susan."

After she got off the phone, Nina tried to piece together how this last pregnancy of Susan's fit into her puzzling death. There were so many ways it could go. Maybe it had been this man's child and he had killed her in a murderous rage after finding out she had done away with the fetus. Possible, but not likely, Nina thought. Most men one ran across these days were only too glad to suggest a trip to the clinic. Any male proprietary feelings about unborn children seemed to belong to religious zealots and parties to contracts with surrogate mothers.

The more likely scenario was that Susan, still emotionally reeling from having to undergo yet another abortion, got herself into a situation that was more dangerous than she realized. Blinded and numbed from terminating her pregnancy, she failed to sense the potential for danger that the situation afforded. Whether or not the murderer was the father was really besides the point. Susan must have been quite a mess, no matter whose it was.

That was especially clear when you knew that Susan Gold was someone who had come of age reading *Our Bodies, Ourselves*. And always used yogurt instead of monostat cream for yeast infections. And relied on cranberry juice instead of sulfa drugs whenever her urinary tract acted up. And yet she had chosen to have a general anaesthetic during an abortion. It wasn't like her. Nina had been through this with her before, and she was sure that Susan had always had a local.

Last time, Susan had said something about never wanting to have to live through this again. She must have decided that giving up consciousness would make it easier to live through. Well, she had lived through the abortion, but not much longer. And Nina sensed that despite the general anaesthesia, this last surgical procedure had taken a toll that Susan could not have anticipated.

# Chapter
# Twenty-six

When Nina got home from work on Monday, there was a message on her answering machine from someone named Clinton Klein. Apparently Nina had answered his ad and he was interested in getting together. Nina was relieved. She couldn't bear the thought of all of those cleverly cut and pasted responses going entirely to waste.

When she called him back, Clinton Klein explained that he was a gynecologist, doing a year's fellowship at Mount Sinai. He had a slight twang, what sounded like a southern accent. Another out-of-town Jew, thought Nina. She hoped he was better looking than Irwin Smolkowitz. She arranged to meet him for a drink on the East Side, near his apartment.

He was the only man at the bar when she walked in, and he was much better looking than Irwin. But an out-of-town Jew he definitely was not, unless he had been adopted. His facial features were clearly those of a Gentile.

She couldn't help herself. The first thing she said, after she sat down and had ordered a Heineken, was "how do you spell your last name?"

"C-L-I-N-E. Like Patsy."

"And how do you pronounce it?" she asked.

"The regular way."

"Like the department store?"

"What department store is that?" he asked. His arrival in New York clearly postdated the demise of S. Klein's. To him, Nina thought, Union Square was probably nothing more than a glorified front yard for Zeckendorf Towers. Its history of anarchists and communists and bargain-basement coats had eluded him. He probably thought it was called Union Square because it marked the unification of Broadway and Park Avenue South.

"There used to be a department store called Klein's in Union Square. What kind of a name is Cline?" She tried to sound polite.

"White trash," he said.

"Oh, I see."

"It's common where I come from," he continued. "There are Clines all over Kentucky and Tennessee."

"So is that your background? White trash?" At least he wasn't pretentious. But he said it with a defiant, rather than a humorous edge.

"Yeah, as far back as I can trace it. My family always farmed, but my father moved on to coal mining. Strip mining, that is. There's not too much deep coal mining in northeast Kentucky."

"But you said you went to school in New England."

"Wesleyan undergrad and then Tufts Medical."

"I don't get it."

"I was a mutant." He smiled and started to seem a little warmer. "There's usually at least one in every small town. The kind of kid that makes the teachers feel like they finally hit pay dirt. They polish you up and make you strut your stuff and if you're lucky, you don't have a nervous breakdown during your freshman year on whatever campus decided to snap you up."

"Was college that awful?"

"Not really. Wesleyan is a liberal place where the student body were open-minded enough to find me interesting. I taught them all the correct pronunciation of Appalachia. The third syllable is pronounced like door latch, you know."

"No, I didn't know."

"Actually, I had a pretty good time there. It was more fun than medical school, anyway."

"Did you consider going back to Kentucky to practice medicine?" Nina asked.

"Not for a minute. I knew I wouldn't end up back home, from the minute I first got out of there—the summer after my junior year in high school."

"What happened then?"

"I was accepted into a science summer program for high school juniors. I got to spend a couple of months in Southern California."

"You had a good time, huh?"

"At first I was a little intimidated by the sheer mental prowess I was surrounded by. I had been used to being the only really smart kid around. But then I discovered something that I was better at than the others. Something that the science nerds hadn't conquered yet."

"And that was?"

"Sex." Clinton Cline leaned back and grinned. "That's one thing the mountains are good for. Not only the mountains, but the South too. Kentucky's not part of the South. You know that don't you?"

"Okay. Kentucky's not part of the South," Nina said, trying to sound agreeable.

"Anyway, while you kids up north are fiddling with the buttons on your electronics equipment, we're out rutting in the fields. It gives us a head start."

"And you don't find that you burn out too soon?"

"Are you kidding?" he said. "At the point that you guys are having your mid-life crises, we're just getting warmed up."

"Come on." Nina sounded more dubious than she actually was. She had always felt that becoming sexually active was something like learning how to swim. If you didn't do it at an early age, you could never be really good at it. She felt that the natural athletes started young and the rest of the world spent their life playing catch-up.

Cline seemed like a natural sexual athlete. It wasn't anything external, although he was good-looking enough. He was just terrifically sexy in that way that couldn't be fabricated. One of those guys that you think about going to bed with the minute you meet them. And if his crooked smile and lascivious eyes weren't enough to prompt the thought, the fact that he was a gynecologist was guaranteed to drive it home.

Nina knew that she was not going to jump into bed with Clinton Cline. For one thing, she had just spent the night with Patrick. And the days of changing bed partners without having time to reinsert your diaphragm were over. She had a feeling that she might have a hard time even sustaining a sexually active state for a prolonged period of time. Being promiscuous was way out of her current range.

But her obsession with Patrick was not enough to dull her sexual responsiveness to Cline. In her experience, one thing had little to do with another. She had found that there was no such thing as sexual fulfillment. You were never really full. There was always room for more. She believed that in most cases a cheating spouse had less to do with problems in the conjugal bed and more to do with the nature of the stimulus that had just crossed that spouse's path.

Of course, there were also the hard-core cheaters, people like Gary Hart and Jack Kennedy, who could no sooner keep their hands off of a hot stimulus than Nina could eat half a piece of cheesecake and put the rest in the refrigerator for tomorrow. These guys could be spotted a mile away. For one thing, they seemed to have fuller heads of hair than other men their age. Maybe it was strictly hormones after all. The women were harder to spot. Sometimes they wore their blouses open an extra button, but mostly they were invisible.

Clinton Cline would—inevitably, once he was married—develop into a compulsive cheater. He had the sexual confidence and full head of hair of Hart and Kennedy. His impressive mop had been sculpted into a handsome wedge, modified enough to make him look au courant without appearing gay. His clothes displayed the same delicate balance. He wore a leather jacket that was a rugged, heterosexual brown and hit his hips low enough to avoid any connotations. He was quite an attractive specimen. She bet his patients never put off *their* yearly pap smears. They probably marched in every six months.

He pulled a small plastic bottle from the pocket of his leather jacket. "My left lens has been bothering me lately," he said as he squeezed a few drops into his eye.

Susan's checklist appeared in Nina's mind's eye. Clinton Cline was perfect: great clothes, a fabulous haircut, and a good build. And contact lenses. But wait, Nina told herself, you've still got one square uncovered.

"Do you ever go hiking?" she said, too excited right now to not get straight to the point.

"Are you kidding?" he said. "I live to hike." Now she had it. Five across. Bingo.

# Chapter
# Twenty-seven

She wriggled away from Clinton Cline as soon as she could. She was in a desperate panic to call Williams. But the phone rang and rang. It was his day off, said the sergeant who finally answered. Maybe he could be found if it was really urgent. No, Nina admitted. It could wait. After all, it was doubtful that a gynecological fellow at Mount Sinai would suddenly disappear.

She ran off to catch an eight o'clock aerobics class. Normally, she hated to exercise that late, especially with alcohol and peanuts polluting her system. But she was too hyped up to sit around with last week's *New Yorker* or the TV. The only watchable thing on at this time was usually on Channel Thirteen, which had deemed eight p.m. as its nature hour. And she was certainly too jumpy to sit through lyrical, protracted descriptions of kangaroos caring for their young. You had to be really mellow to watch that stuff. Nature specials were something like a modern reincarnation of the lava lamp.

The class seemed to calm her down somewhat. It wasn't until toward the end, when she was in that contemplative state of stretching out her Achilles' tendon, that she started again to obsess about Clinton Cline. By the time she got back to the locker room, she had decided to see if she could find Williams after all. She was digging into her purse for a quarter, when someone called to her from across the room. It was Gwen, sitting on a bench, pulling on a tiger-print unitard. The two women hugged. "When did you get back?" Nina asked.

"An hour ago. Literally. All I could think of was running straight to the gym."

"Did you have a good time?"

"Europe was wonderful. We had the best time, but my body completely fell apart." Gwen's body had a long way to go to get to apart. It looked like it was holding together quite well. Gwen had the kind of body that *Sports Illustrated* might pay a lot of money to let them photograph for their swimsuit edition. And she had a glorious full head of long red hair that was set off nicely by the brown-and-orange tiger print. Gwen was the best-looking woman Nina knew. Also the richest. Life was filled with such coincidences.

As Gwen pulled on her legwarmers, Nina internally debated how to bring up the topic of Susan's death. It was clear that Gwen hadn't heard, otherwise she wouldn't be smiling so cheerfully as she wrapped that adorable little belt around her tiny waist. Someday Nina would like to be the kind of woman who actually shopped for exercise accessories. It was all she could do to buy a new Coach bag every other year.

She decided not to beat around the bush. To tell her swiftly and simply. "Susan's dead," Nina said. "She was murdered."

Gwen sunk to the bench. "Tell me everything," she said in a flat voice.

"She was found strangled to death on a hiking trail upstate. They don't know how it happened or who did it or why. She had told me that she was going hiking that weekend with a new boyfriend, but no one knows who he is."

Gwen started to cry. "Oh my God, this is all my fault," she sobbed.

It wasn't exactly the response Nina had expected. "Your fault," she said. "Are you crazy?"

"I told her to confront him."

"Him? Him who?"

"She never told me his name. She was superstitious about being jinxed."

Now it was Nina's turn. "Tell *me* everything."

"Let's get out of here," Gwen said, "and go someplace where we can talk."

"Do you want to come over to my place?" Nina said comfortingly.

"Good idea. Then I'll just go home and do Jane Fonda before I go to bed." The woman was hardcore, Nina thought. She hadn't gotten to where she was by not concentrating. Gwen stuffed her clothing into her gym bag, put on her gym shoes, and threw her jacket on over her unitard. She was another one who could run around the street without pants. Like Susan. Nina felt the tiniest flicker of resentment. Why had Susan confided in Gwen instead of her? And why could some women get away with walking the streets practically in their underwear, while Nina had to consider one crummy pair of tap pants a high-risk venture?

"Do you need a drink?" Nina asked, once they were settled on her couch.

"Do you have any herbal tea?" Of course Nina

had herbal tea. Boxes and boxes of it. Red zinger, lemon zinger, orange zinger, all the zingers. She was the kind of woman who had boxes of herbal teas, but when seeking comfort would head straight for the Jameson. Or the leftover cream cheese.

Nina called out her inventory of herbal tea. Gwen settled on cinnamon rose. "Do you want something to eat?" Nina knew what the answer was going to be. She rarely saw Gwen actually ingest anything. She seemed to exist primarily on a diet of marinated seaweed, which she claimed was nature's most healthful food. She was always trying to get everyone else to increase their intake of sea vegetables. Nina stubbornly clung to the antiquated notion of land vegetables.

"No thanks," Gwen said on cue.

"Do you want honey in your tea?"

"Do you have any barley malt?" Apparently honey was no longer considered a health food.

"No, I don't have any barley malt."

"You should really get some."

"Give me a break," Nina said. "Do you want honey or not?"

"It's okay. I think I have some sucanate in my purse."

Nina had never heard of the stuff, but she wasn't in the mood to initiate one of Gwen's nutritional lectures. She let it pass.

Gwen rummaged around and retrieved a packet. She emptied it into the cup Nina handed her, stirred, sipped, and sighed. "I can't believe this happened," she said and stared into her tea.

"You said something about telling Susan to confront this man. What did you mean?"

"Well, she complained to me that he was being a little mysterious. For example, when he called her it was always from the office or his car phone, never from his house. And when she called him at home, she always got his answering machine. Susan started to think that the number he had given her wasn't really his home number at all. Which made her think that he might be married. Also, she had never seen where he lived. But he was so available that she thought she was being paranoid. She figured since he was always willing to spend Saturday night with her, he couldn't have been married."

"And what was your diagnosis?"

"I told her that his availability didn't mean anything, since some guys can get away with telling their wives that they're going on a business trip and stay with their mistresses for the weekend."

"Did this guy travel on business?"

"Susan didn't tell me exactly what he did, but she did say that it was conceivable that his work could require him to go out of town for a weekend."

"So you thought he was married?"

"I thought it was very possible. I told her she should confront him with the evidence. Ask him why was he always calling her from his car phone? Why had she never seen his house? How come she always got his answering machine? But I advised her to be somewhat low key about it. You know Susan. She tended toward the histrionic."

"Yeah," Nina said. "She could get pretty worked up. I can just see her telling him 'leave your wife, or else.' Do you think she was that serious about him?"

"I think she wanted this one badly."

"My mother said something about Susan recently. About her tenacity. That when she decided that she wanted something, she drove people crazy until she got it. Do you agree?"

"Absolutely. Susan must have driven this guy crazy, don't you think?"

"Well, he couldn't have been too balanced to begin with," Nina said. "A simple 'can it, Susan' would have sufficed. He didn't have to kill her."

"Didn't you ever feel like killing her?"

"I didn't have as emotionally charged a relationship with her as you did, Gwen." The thought occurred to Nina that perhaps Gwen hadn't really been in Europe. Perhaps she had been hiding out after murdering Susan. Nina tried to remember whether she had received any postcards from Europe. But that was ridiculous. Gwen never sent postcards. And if Gwen was going to strangle Susan, she wouldn't do it on top of a mountain. Gwen's idea of a day hike was walking across the park to have brunch at the Stanhope.

"Did you know that she had had an abortion right before this happened?" Nina asked Gwen.

"Yes. But it wasn't his," she said. "Susan was already pregnant when she met this guy."

"Whose was it?" Nina immediately regretted asking the question. It seemed intrusive, like a gossip columnist assigned to write a posthumous article.

Gwen took a moment to answer. "She didn't tell me his name. Someone unavailable. At work."

"Unavailable in what way?" asked Nina. "Married?"

"I'm not sure. He might have been married. She wouldn't say. He could have been a priest, for all I know. She kept saying 'Out of the question. It's out of the question,' every time I suggested she make it a permanent arrangement. I would guess married."

Gwen would, Nina thought, based on her first husband's track record. "So she was pretty clear about her decision to have an abortion?"

"Are you kidding?" Gwen gave her a derisive

look. "Pretty clear? What do you think? She agonized over it nonstop."

Of course, thought Nina. These things were especially hard because in public you had to keep up such a positive pro-choice stance. In the midst of such a virulent political climate, there was no room for emotion. Not that Nina, or any woman she knew, had any doubt at all that a woman's right to choose was sacrosanct. But that didn't make the choice any easier. "How did she finally decide?" she asked.

"First someone at work got suspicious and confronted her about the affair."

"How did they figure it out?"

"It was interesting. Susan said that no one had a clue that anything was going on until another nurse stumbled across a stack of interoffice envelopes that Susan had on her desk. You know the kind."

Nina's office was too small for such things, but she knew what Gwen meant. They were oversized and manila and the front was divided into little rectangles, and you crossed out the name of the last recipient and wrote in the name of the new addressee in the rectangle below. "Yes, I know what you mean."

"Well," Gwen continued, "this other nurse had run out of interoffice envelopes and there were none in the supply closet. So she came by Susan's desk to ask her if she had any. 'Sure,' Susan said, 'I have a whole stack.' And handed them over. They had all been addressed to Susan and had piled up before she had a chance to use them again. This nurse flipped through the stack after Susan handed them to her and noticed right away that they had all been sent to her from the same person."

"How did she know?" Nina asked, but then figured it out. "Wait, I get it. The addressee above

Susan's name, the one that was crossed out, was the same on every envelope. Right?''

"Exactly. Very good. According to Susan, this guy would send her cute little notes and clippings through the interoffice mail all the time. As a romantic gesture. So this nurse asked Susan, Why all the mail from so-and-so? What's going on? And Susan, being a couple of weeks pregnant and in emotional and hormonal turmoil, burst into tears and confessed everything. Well, this nurse was a tough-mama type who had been around. And she told Susan that she had always thought that this guy was a no-good womanizer and had the distinct impression that this was not the first time he had been in such a situation. And from what she understood, he had, on a previous occasion, acted like a real shithead. In her opinion, the best thing for Susan to do would be to extract herself from this mess as soon as possible.''

Nina reeled slightly on Gwen's emphasis on the word *extract*. It had such clear abortive connotations. "And that's when she decided to end the pregnancy?" she asked.

"Not quite. She was still waffling when this hiking guy answered her ad. Apparently they hit it off tremendously well and Susan saw great promise.''

"Except for the fact that she was pregnant with someone else's baby," Nina said.

"Right. So she thought she'd give herself another chance. But it was clear that it was taking a great toll on her. She kept saying that this would be the last one. And she decided to be put under. She didn't want to have to relive it, which she was afraid would happen if she only had a local.''

Another chance. Nina knew the feeling. A fresh start. Wipe yourself clean of all the smudge marks and tell yourself, this time it was going to be different. The urge to re-invent oneself for a new man was always compelling. As if you could become a virgin again. There was always a tendency to purge oneself, to remove whatever corrosive build-up had accumulated. The leg waxing, the facial peeling, the ingestion of food with diarrhetic properties. Nina remembered sitting in a sauna once an hour before a second date, with garbage bags wrapped around her legs. Just a few more drops of sweat and she'd be reborn. She stayed in too long and had spent the evening lightheaded and nauseated. She'd sworn off all purge-related activities that night. But she could understand how Susan had felt. Could she blame her for deciding to undertake that ultimate purge? What a state of mind it must have left her in, so invested in succeeding with a man she didn't even know.

Gwen spoke Nina's thoughts. "You can imagine how she felt after the abortion. The pressure it put on her to make things work out with this man at all costs. I could tell, although she was strangely silent about it."

"Silent doesn't sound like Susan," Nina said, thinking of all those years of huge long-distance phone bills. It was too bad that the Internal Revenue Service did not consider obsessing a tax deductible item.

"Sometimes she'd say 'I think this might be it' in a breathless sort of way and then stop short. Like she was knocking on wood."

Funny, Nina thought. Susan had not been big on kine ahoras. That was one of the things Nina had loved about her. She'd indulge in all sorts of fantasies, going on and on for hours about what if this and what if that. And yet she'd revealed none of this to Nina. She must have been hurting bad. Usually the pain and obsession was directly proportional to the amount of time you spent on the phone. But past a certain point, when it got too painful, even Susan would clam up.

"Anyway," Gwen continued, "it was obvious that she was harboring very high hopes for this new relationship. And the little she told me about him sounded good. Except for her suspicions about his marital status, which, I had to admit to her, sounded as if they were based on reality. She tried to keep telling herself that a man who goes out on Saturday night can't be married. But we both knew that wasn't necessarily the case."

"What finally convinced her?"

"The perfume."

"Perfume?" Nina noticed that the hair on her arms was standing up.

"She told me that he had given her perfume as a gift. And was insistent that she stop wearing her regular stuff. What was that stuff she wore?"

"Obsession," Nina said.

"It would be, wouldn't it? Anyway, he told her to stop wearing Obsession and switch to this stuff. As soon as she said that, I knew he was married. Or at least living with someone."

"I don't get it."

"That's how I figured out Charles was cheating on me." Charles, Gwen's first husband, was currently living in Marin County with his new wife, a flight attendant named Samantha. "You know I'm completely devoted to Chanel Number Five. It's hopelessly old-fashioned, I admit, but I like it. I haven't worn anything else in decades. So when I started to smell a scent that wasn't Chanel Number Five clinging to Charles' suits, I knew he was rubbing up against someone else."

"Really? I didn't know that."

"I thought I'd spare my friends the more sordid

details of my divorce." Gwen nervously ran her hands through her hair and bit her lip. "Since then," she continued, "I've heard the same tale from other spurned wives. It seems that a really experienced guy, a professional cheater, knows enough to get his girlfriend to switch to his wife's fragrance. I explained this to Susan and she found that pretty convincing. She called me that next day to tell me that she was working herself up to confronting him."

"Gwen, she didn't happen to mention what kind of perfume he gave her, did she?"

"She did, but I can't quite remember the name. It was made by a company that manufactures skin care products. Everyone's branching out into perfume, you know. Clothing designers, movie stars, everyone."

"Do you remember the name of the skin care company?"

"I'm pretty sure it was Prescriptives."

Nina got up from the couch, walked into her bedroom and picked up the bottle of Calyx from her bureau. She turned it upside down. There, on the bottom, was a tiny label. And there it was, on the tiny label, in tiny print. But big enough to read: Prescriptives.

So that was what Susan had wanted that another woman had—her husband. And that husband happened to be the man that Nina had spent last Friday night with.

The phone rang. Nina let the machine kick in. It was Irwin Smolkowitz. Nina didn't pick up.

# Chapter
# Twenty-eight

She felt like she couldn't go through with it. As she watched the street through her window, waiting for Patrick's car, she half hoped he would never come.

But it was all set up. Williams had found Gwen credible; self-absorbed and narcissistic, he confided to Nina later, but credible. His plan was to simulate the conditions of Susan's murder as closely as possible—to send Nina off hiking with Patrick and see what happened when she confronted him about his marital status. Her instructions were to be very insistent. And Williams would follow close behind. Those were the two weakest plot elements, Nina's ability to be insistent and Williams' ability to follow close behind. He was bringing plenty of back-up, of course. And he had assured her that he had chosen only those members of the force with the highest level of cardiovascular fitness. But she couldn't get rid of the image of Williams, huffing and puffing, stumbling across her corpse.

She had hoped for rain, anything to put this off. But this morning was beautiful, with only a few wispy cirrus clouds. Too bad this was going to be their last date. Not only did Nina and Patrick have great sex together, they also had great weather.

Looking out the window, she wondered whether she should have known he was married. He hadn't shown any of the usual traits—checking his watch compulsively or jumping out of bed at two in the morning or sneaking off to restaurant phone booths when he was supposed to be in the bathroom. But then, he had the kind of job that lent itself to disappearing. One can't necessarily investigate just Monday through Friday between nine and five. And Gwen had figured out the perfume angle only because of personal experience. Unlike Gwen, Nina had not spent most of her adult life as someone's wife or mistress. She couldn't have expected herself to have picked up on that one. The only thing she should have been suspicious about was the green nylon duffel bag in the back of his car. Now it made sense. If he had told his wife he was going out of town on business, he would have had to pack. And he had been so testy when she had asked him about it, she should have known something was up.

There he was. As soon as she caught a glimpse of his Subaru wagon, she pulled on her jacket, hurriedly locked the door behind her, and ran downstairs to meet him. Now that it was clear she couldn't put this off, she wanted to get it over with as soon as possible. Patrick and Daisy were already on the sidewalk when she emerged from her building. The dog jumped up to greet her before Patrick could get to her. She held on to Daisy for as long as she could, trying to avoid having to deal with him.

"I see I'm competing with my own dog," he said.

"Don't be silly," she said, trying to breathe normally.

"Don't I get a kiss?"

She turned her face to him. Kissing a man who might murder you later in the day wasn't really that different from kissing most other men, Nina thought, as she relaxed into the act. No matter whom you were kissing, you were always trying to put out of your mind what might happen as soon as the kiss was over.

"So, are we going to do Slide today?" she asked. Nina and Patrick were planning to climb Slide Mountain, where Susan's body had been found. Williams had carefully poured over trail maps of the area, so that she could be kept track of at all times.

"I thought we'd do Ledges instead." Ledges was another popular trail, not far from Slide Mountain. But far enough. Nina pictured herself lying dead on the ascent to Ledges while the New York City police force frantically combed Slide Mountain for her body.

"I really had my heart set on Slide." Nina tried for a pretty pout. "I did Ledges last year and I haven't been up Slide in ages." She barely knew what she was talking about, but she tried to sound convincing. It wasn't really hard, she realized. It was like being in court, that was all.

"Okay, if that's what you want. Slide it is," he said. Nina felt like she had just gotten a benign diagnosis after a biopsy. She had a chance of surviving.

In the car she felt the way she had felt at the window. She wished they'd never get there. She often had these feelings, even when the event looming on the horizon caused only mild apprehension. She would sit in transit, praying that the subway would break down or that a sudden blizzard would appear and dump enough snow to paralyze all traffic. She would fantasize that the crosstown bus would be hijacked or the person she was on her way to meet would get struck down in a crosswalk. The image that most often recurred, practically every weekday morning, was of the Civil Courthouse suddenly exploding and flames quickly devouring every document in the clerk's office before the fire engines even got there. As a teenager she had often imagined the same thing happening to the Bronx High School of Science, on days when her biology lab book was due or a physics exam was scheduled.

Today, as they headed up the Henry Hudson Parkway, she pictured the George Washington Bridge snapping in two. And once they were safely over the bridge and onto the Palisades Parkway, she pictured Patrick slumped over the wheel, dead of a sudden heart attack, the car off on the side of the road.

That would make this whole thing moot. She knew she longed for mootness far too often. In court she always scrutinized the summons and complaint longingly, hoping for a defect that would get the action dismissed. Instead of charging in there like some of her colleagues, anxious to try this motherfucker. Today she should be relishing the thought of avenging Susan's murder. Go for it, she usually tried telling herself, instead of fantasizing about mootness by catastrophe. Grab life by the balls. Smell the roses. Drink deep. Taste it. Chew it. Go for the gusto. You only go round once. But no matter how many times she mentally sang the lyrics to "Cabaret," she continually found herself, no matter what her destination, hoping she'd never get there.

Williams had said that he would send a car to follow them, just in case they never got to Slide. But as far as she could see, they weren't being tailed. Whether this was due to skillfulness or ineptness, she couldn't tell. So she was relieved when they pulled into the parking lot and she saw Williams leaning against a car, talking to two men and a woman. All four were dressed for hiking, but they each looked a little bit wrong. Williams had chosen khaki pants and a gray down vest. The word elephantine came to mind. One of the other men, a tall redhead, wore a green satin Celtics jacket. Not only did the guy look like he was pretending to be Larry Bird, but the combination of the red hair and green satin was too loud for the hiking trail, where earth tones generally prevailed. The other guy looked a little more normal, in jeans and a sixty-forty windbreaker, but his face spelled cop. He had one of those closely trimmed mustaches that were designed not to look good, but to meet department regulations.

The woman was one of those old-fashioned lesbians who bought their pants in the men's department and kept their hair very short. This cavalier attitude always amazed Nina who, with wide hips and a small head, worked hard to reverse her pyramidal curse. She shopped hard and long for pants that crept high up her waist and trained her hair to fill up as many cubic inches around her head as possible. The idea was to create the impression of an inverted triangle. It was a universally accepted fashion statement. So she was always slightly in awe of women who defiantly ignored this geometric theorem, as if to say that being well grounded was more important than anything else. That they had no desire to look like a peony—all head and no foliage, fluttering in the wind, about to flop over at any moment. That it was better to be a shrub that could survive even a tornado with its roots still in the ground.

Of course, Nina knew there was a whole new school of lesbians who had personal shoppers at Lord and Taylor and who wore Bruno Magli shoes. But the woman who stood talking to Williams was the sturdy traditional sort, which gave Nina confidence.

"Nice day," Patrick said to the group, as they passed on their way to the trail head. It was a cardinal rule of hiking: You could be the rudest New Yorker, closed up as tight as a clam shell, but as soon as you strapped on your day pack, you had to do a decent imitation of a Midwestern housewife at a church supper.

Williams' plan was to have Nina and Patrick climb up Slide and start back down again. Williams and his partner were to follow them to the top, wait for them to leave and then follow them down. The other two would, instead of following them all the way to the top, hang back a bit and stay ahead of them on the descent. That way Patrick and Nina would stay sandwiched between the two pairs of cops. According to the trail maps, there was a steep descent from the summit, followed by an isolated wooded area in the deep notch between Slide and Cornell mountains. As soon as they got to these woods, Nina was to initiate a confrontation. When she actually would get him to threaten her, the two teams of cops would close in and intervene.

The hike was quite beautiful. It was easy enough to pretend that there was no subplot to the day. But Nina was wearing a wire. It was a tiny little thing, under her shirt, but it gave an air of reality to the expedition. Whenever she felt that she had imagined all this, she pressed her arm up against the tiny microphone.

The approach to the summit climbed steeply. When the open rock top of the mountain came into view, Nina got jumpier. Right below the huge rock, Patrick stopped to point out a metal tablet embedded in the ground. "In Memoriam," Nina read, and for one insane moment she imagined it had been put there for her, in advance. She forced herself to read the rest. This is what it said:

## In Memoriam

### John Burroughs

Who in his early writings introduced Slide Mountain to the world. He made many visits to this peak and slept several nights beneath this rock. This region is the scene of many of his essays. Here the works of man dwindle in the heart of the Southern Catskills.

That was precisely how Nina felt at the moment. Dwindling in the heart of the Southern Catskills.

They settled down on the rock to have lunch. Nina pulled cheese sandwiches and apples from her day pack. Patrick pulled a water bottle and a hip flask from his. Despite the circumstances, Nina felt a flush of pleasure at the sight of the flask. She had always felt that there was something romantically dangerous about hip flasks. Well, she had been right, hadn't she? That was her problem. She was still looking for men with hip flasks instead of men with retirement funds.

She looked around the deserted rocky summit. Williams was nowhere to be seen. She had to assume he was waiting in the woods below.

Patrick handed her the flask. "What's in it?" she asked.

"Jameson. Our drink."

She took a healthy hit. It might slow down her reflexes. But then again, it might calm her down to a functional state. "I could get used to this," she said.

"To what?"

"Drinking Jameson with you. On a regular basis."
Patrick smiled. "I hope you do."

"I don't think so."

"Why not?"

"You're married, aren't you?" Why had she said
that? She wasn't proceeding according to the plan.
She was supposed to wait until Williams had appeared and she and Patrick had gone back down to
the woods. It was true that she wanted to get the
whole thing over with, but this was ridiculous.

"What makes you think that?"

Don't be crazy, she said to herself. Drop it and go
back to the plan. Tell him never mind, or something.
She could still get out of this. But something was
making her push on. "I can tell."

"Oh really?"

"Yes, really. And I think it's awful. Someone
should tell your wife."

"Nina, don't say anything you're going to be sorry
about."

"Why? What's going to happen to me?"

"You're being a very silly girl."

"So you're not denying it?"

"I think we should go back now."

"No, I want you to tell me the truth."

"It's really none of your business."

"None of my business? It is so my goddamn business. And it's your wife's goddamn business too. I've
found out your home address, you know, even
though you have an unlisted phone number. And I'm
going to write to her and tell her what you're doing."
She knew she was being insane. Williams was nowhere to be seen. But she seemed incapable of stopping her performance. Because it was no longer a
performance. She was trembling with rage.

"You're not going to contact my wife." His voice was very controlled.

"How are you going to stop me?"

"Believe me, Nina, I'll take whatever steps necessary to stop you. Don't think I won't."

"Are you threatening me?" She didn't give him a chance to answer. "This is what happened with Susan, isn't it?"

"Susan?" He sounded shocked. So was Nina, actually. Mentioning Susan had not been in the plan.

"Susan Gold. Who you strangled to death. On this very trail."

"I'm sorry you know about that, Nina. Sorry for you." He grabbed her roughly.

Nina wondered if this was the right time to scream. If Williams was nearby, it would be helpful. If not, it might be a mistake. She could very conceivably be killed in the next five minutes. She hadn't felt this threatened since the time she accidently fell asleep on the Seventh Avenue uptown express at midnight and had woken up at 110th and Lenox. Well, at least the murder of Nina Fischman wouldn't go into the annals of unsolved mysteries.

Suddenly the grip he had on her went limp. His hand fell away and he turned his back to her and took a few steps. His shoulders shuddered in what seemed to be a sob. He pulled at his hair. He turned back to her with tears in his eyes. "I still can't believe it happened," he said. "Of course, I never meant it to. I still don't understand the whole thing."

Nina was disconcerted. The scenario had flipped quickly from what seemed like a murder attempt to a therapy session. It was her fate, she guessed. Life imitates therapy. She couldn't think of an appropriate response, so she stood silently and let him continue.

"We were here, and we were having a great time.

It was a particularly passionate afternoon. And all of a sudden she pulled away, stared me straight in the eye and said 'fuck you.' And then she starts screaming all this stuff along the lines of 'you're married, aren't you, you fucking asshole' and she's hyperventilating and her eyes are popping out of her head. I try to calm her down, but she starts screaming 'don't touch me, get away from me.' So I start walking away from her and she throws a rock at me. Then I lost it. I went back over to her and started shaking her and screaming. And she was screaming back and trying to claw my face. I remember thinking that I had to get her to stop screaming. I really don't remember much else. The next thing I remember is seeing my hands around her neck and her head go limp."

Nina felt a tear run down her cheek. Patrick noticed. "Believe me," he said, "you have nothing to worry about. It was an act of pure rage. I'm no good at the premeditated stuff. Never have been."

Nina quashed an impulse to empathize. "But I assume," Patrick continued, "that it is your intention to see to it that this ruins my life." He reached into his pocket and pulled out his Swiss Army knife. He unfolded a blade and pointed it in her direction. "Is this the way things are supposed to play out?" he said. "That you're supposed to say that you're going to see to it that I spend the rest of my life behind bars? And I'm supposed to plunge this into your chest and run off to Mexico and spend the rest of my life in a tequila-soaked cloud?"

The sight of the blade was chilling, but the look on his face was such a mix of despair and sarcasm that her fear subsided. They stood there for a minute, fixed in what seemed to be a scene from a play. The silence was broken by a woman's voice.

"Drop that knife." Nina was glad to hear the

voice, but it wasn't one she recognized. Nina turned around and there were two elderly women with binoculars hanging around their necks. The taller of the two spoke. "Just what do you think you're doing?"

"Lady, this is really none of your business," Patrick said. But he threw the knife to the ground.

The four of them stood awkwardly for a moment, staring at each other. Finally Williams appeared with the guy in the Celtics jacket. They both had guns drawn. "Police," Williams said. He lowered his gun and pulled out his badge.

"Oh my God," one of the old ladies said.

"Everything's under control," Williams continued. "Check him." The redhead pulled Patrick aside and patted him down.

"Where the hell were you?" Nina said, her voice shaking and tears forming.

"We were waiting for you to start on your way down. Then we were going to pass you and follow you down. That was the plan."

"It was?"

"Yes it was. And you know damn well that you weren't supposed to get him angry until you had gone back down to the woods. What the hell was that all about?"

"I don't know. I just started screaming at him and I couldn't stop. I guess I was in a hurry to get it over with."

"Nina, when you're investigating a murder, you need to exhibit a little impulse control."

"I'm not always good at that. Sometimes I eat after dinner."

"Officer," one of the old ladies said, "do you need us or can we go?"

"I'd like to at least get your names and addresses in case we need you for questioning."

"Certainly."

"And thank you for your assistance," he added politely.

The woman turned to Nina. "We're birders," she said. "We don't miss anything." And she held up her binoculars for emphasis.

# Chapter
# Twenty-nine

Discretionary children. That's what the demographers call anything after the second baby." Nina pressed up against the glass to examine her new nephew more closely. "Of course," she went on, "I consider all children to be discretionary. If I considered them mandatory, my life would make no sense." She paused. "Because I don't have any," she added for further clarification.

"I know you don't have any," Ida said.

"I guess you do know that." Nina rapped on the partition that separated her from twenty swaddled infants. "What's your name?" she called to the one on the left in the bassinet marked *Rubin*. But he was fast asleep.

"They've narrowed it down to Ethan or Evan," Ida said. Apparently the Park Slope crowd had moved on from Joshua and Jason to the vowels. "And they're having a bris."

"You're kidding. They didn't have a bris for Jared."

"No, but your sister's gotten more religious lately."

As if Nina hadn't noticed. What had begun as a convenient location for the children's swimming lessons had mushroomed into a full-scale temple membership and Friday-night candle lighting ceremonies. And now a bris.

Nina thought about it. Judaism made sense for Laura and Ken and the three little Rubins. Institutions—including marriage, and now, religion—seemed to afford her sister a measure of comfort. That's what institutions were supposed to do. Instead of making you feel like you wanted to kick someone in the shins.

Was Nina eternally damned to adolescent purgatory? Late adolescent purgatory, actually, where she could see the validity of conformity but somehow not be able to take the final step and embrace it. But she lacked the soul of a true rebel. It would be easier if she could just get behind herself, committing strongly to a life of nonconformity. But getting behind herself was a complicated dance, which seemed to result only in Nina running around in circles.

She wished she could go one way or the other. A feisty feminist with fire in her eyes, coldly and clinically dissecting daily events in an attempt to distill the truth. Or a dreamy young mom, with eyes focussed somewhere over the horizon, responding with a sleepy "Hmmmm?" every time you said something to them. As if the marijuana haze of twenty years ago had suddenly redescended in the brownstones of Park Slope and the backyards of Tenafly.

One way or the other. Well, the magazines said that a woman could have many lives. A stoned-out nursing mother could become a fiery-eyed feminist later on, when the kids were safely off to college. Ida, in her own tortured way, had managed to have pulled this off. But Nina's life seemed to have no phases. Sure, the panic of not having done your homework had metamorphosed into the panic of not wanting to bring a case to trial. And the humiliation of not having anyone to eat lunch with in the school cafeteria had evolved into the lack of a brownstone, and of a bris to have in it. But mostly it had all felt the same. There were only so many decades you could spend whining about not having a boyfriend. Two was pushing it. Three was absolutely over the limit. And she was going on her third.

Nina looked at baby boy Rubin. He was lucky to be part of Laura's little empire. Nina had never felt part of any empire—neither empress nor subject. Rather, she was a free agent, with an ability to slip across borders without anyone noticing. The problem with that status, of course, was that you could just as easily slip into oblivion without anyone noticing.

It wasn't really true that no one would notice. But look at Susan. There had been much weeping and wailing and seven days of shiva, but now everything was pretty much business as usual. But maybe it was like that for everyone, even empresses like her sister. Nina had once heard a story about a young mother who knew she was dying. "Just make sure my kids don't forget me," she kept saying, over and over.

She supposed that everyone must be scared of oblivion, the way everyone was scared of death. No matter how connected you were. Which was probably why it was a natural human impulse to imagine your funeral and do a quick head count.

Maybe it was a universal impulse, but somehow being alone made you feel closer to death. Having your oldest friend killed didn't help, either. "Do you want to see if Laura's up yet?" Ida asked. Her sister had been asleep when they had arrived at the hospital to visit.

"You know what? I think I'm going to head home." Being alone might make you feel closer to death, but being with her family sometimes made her feel closer to suicide. "Send Laura my congratulations."

As she sat on the crosstown bus, Nina thought about Laura's empire. Would the sun ever set on it? The past decade had been a good one for her sister. Was this new one going to be as equally beneficent? It was hard to tell. Her sister was a real '80s person, the way Abbie Hoffman had been a real '60s person and Steve Rubell had been a real '70s person. Instead of a political movement or a drug-laden disco, Laura had created a Kids-R-Us family that typified the past ten years.

Nina had yet to hit her stride in any decade. Maybe the '90s would finally be it for her. The Over Decade. The era of the overeducated, overanalyzed, overweight Jewish woman. While the emperors would be imprisoned for white-collar crime and the empresses would be imprisoned in their brownstones, juggling other people's schedules, the Ninas of the world would be the only ones still functioning.

The phone was ringing when she walked into her apartment. Caught off guard, she answered it.

It was Irwin Smolkowitz. He had been desperate to reach her and had left several messages. Had she gotten them? Why hadn't she returned his calls? He had something important to tell her. He didn't want her to take this personally, he felt that their relationship had a lot of potential, but it was necessary for him to return home to Johannesburg. If she was ever in the area, she should feel free, etc.

She assured him that he would be the first person

she'd call if she ever found herself in South Africa. Then she hung up.

She tallied up her social successes of the recent past. Great sex with a sociopathic killer and a "keep in touch" brush-off from a South African nerd. Not too impressive. And now she couldn't even call Susan to commiserate. The only woman Nina knew with a worse track record than herself was dead because of it. Death by track record.

Nina considered cutting her losses and giving up men. She would become a professional aunt, doting on her sister's kids, knitting little patterned sweaters and taking her niece and nephews to the Museum of Natural History every week. Or maybe she would throw herself into her career, trying cases instead of settling them and scrutinizing every plaintiff for class action potential. She could also start working out at the gym obsessively and try to turn her naturally hypotonic body into a stunning mass of muscle.

The truth was that none of that held much appeal. The law, the gym, her niece and nephews—all were capable of holding her attention for only limited periods of time. Deep down she knew she was never going to give up men. Maybe heterosexuality was a curse, but it was her curse. She supposed she could be a bit more cautious from now on. Marriage material, that's what she should be looking for. On the other hand, look where that got Susan.

The phone rang again. This time she let the machine kick in. It was Williams. "I called to see how you were doing," he said.

She picked up. "I'm here."

"How are you?"

"Truthfully? Feeling sorry for myself."

"That's too bad," Williams said.

"But enjoying it. Self-pity is one of my favorite activities."

"You'll be glad to hear that we're getting very close to an indictment."

"That's great. I've been meaning to ask you something. There was one thing that never made any sense to me. The contact lens discrepancy. Did Patrick wear them or not?"

"Extended wear lenses," Williams said. "He only had to change them once a week."

"Of course. Why didn't I think of that?"

"The guy travelled light."

"He did." Nina thought about Patrick. Everything had made him feel closed in—his office, his marriage. He couldn't even talk on a phone that was attached to the wall. He had gone beyond travelling light. He was a man who had come unplugged. And yet she had fallen for him hard. It made Nina wonder how plugged in she was herself. She had a two-year lease and a one-year gym membership and another six months on her *New Yorker* subscription. And a job that gave her a headache. Were these the ties that bind? It remained unclear.

"Once the grand jury indicts," Williams went on, "I thought we might celebrate."

"We? You mean you and me?"

"Well, I'd invite Patrick, but I don't think he'd come."

Nina realized she was flushed. And she knew what that meant. Hold on, she said to herself. She had just decided to be more cautious. She definitely should not be getting involved with this guy. Not if she was supposed to be looking for marriage material. Williams was a cop, and past fifty, and had already confided in her that his divorced status suited him. On the other hand, his wife and daughter had married

Jews. Maybe he was next. Before she could stop herself, there she went, picturing herself hauling around a beautiful mixed-race infant with golden brown skin and a halo of soft black curls.

"Sure," she said, "let's celebrate. We'll do something fun."

"No hiking, though."

"No, I think the season's over. It is for me, anyway. We'll do something indoors." Too provocative, she noted mentally. Downright flirtatious. So much for impulse control. But what the hell. She had just decided that she was doomed eternally to a life as a practicing heterosexual. As the old joke went, she might as well keep practicing until she got it right.

# SARAH SHANKMAN

# SHE WALKS IN BEAUTY

## A SAMANTHA ADAMS NOVEL

### COMING SOON IN HARDCOVER
### FROM POCKET BOOKS

POCKET
B O O K S